Unconditional

Holly Copella

ISBN: 0997106409
ISBN-13: 978-0-997106404

For Michael Emerson--
whose talent continues to inspire me

ACKNOWLEDGMENTS

Copella Books: First Paperback Edition 2016
Cover Artist: Daniela
SelfPubBookCovers.com/Daniela
Printed by CreateSpace, An Amazon.com Company

PUBLISHER'S NOTE

Chapter One

Flynn Stryker's French colonial plantation style home sat nestled on a large parcel of land on a back road in the middle of nowhere. If there had been neighbors, they'd be envious of the grandeur of the home. The painstakingly refinished home had cascading brick steps leading up to the large front porch. Above the front porch was the second floor terrace in all its grandeur. The yard was professionally landscaped with large, older trees and neatly contained flowerbeds. Within the plantation house, the marble and wood grand foyer contained a beautiful, curved staircase cascading up to the second floor. The cathedral ceiling with its large, second floor window brightened the entire foyer. An attractive, dark-haired woman in her early twenties decorated the staircase railing with holly and ivy. Indy Stryker was regarded by many in town as 'the girl next door'. She had an innocence about her that captured the hearts of many young men, but hers was a classic case of 'looks can be deceiving'.

A slightly older yet equally attractive woman with a slinky body and long, strawberry blonde hair followed Indy up the stairs while attaching large, red bows along the outer railing. Liz Masters was almost ten years Indy's senior, but if events continued along their current path, she would be Indy's stepmother. Indy's father met and fell in love with Liz a little over ten months ago. Liz seemed perfect for Indy's father in every conceivable way. Despite her trim, sexy body, she was a surprisingly good cook, which took some pressure off Indy, who just never quite mastered culinary excellence. Her father moved Liz into the family house prior to his most recent overseas deployment nearly five months ago. Although she felt his moving Liz into the house was rushed, Indy didn't mind the company while her father was away.

The home was lavishly decorated for an extravagant, traditional Christmas. With good reason. It was going be the first Christmas Indy's father would be home since her mother had died five years ago. She wanted everything perfect for her father's return from yet another lengthy, overseas mission. The faint sound of Christmas music echoed along the first floor to help maintain the holiday spirit for the decorating festivities. Liz leaned on the railing overlooking the foyer and drifted out while waiting for Indy to finish another stretch of railing.

"I can't believe he's coming home next week," Liz announced with an almost dreamy sigh while resting her chin on her fist. "I really miss that man."

Indy glanced at her father's attractive girlfriend and hid her smile. She was almost certain her father would be very happy to see Liz as well. Indy would need to locate her noise canceling headphones, so she wouldn't have to hear that joyful reunion during all hours of the night. The thought made her slightly nauseous, but she just wanted her father to be happy.

"I hate when he's gone this long," Indy replied and attempted to conceal her concerns for his safety. "He's always talking about retiring. I wish he'd just do it."

Liz straightened and grinned slyly. "Well, maybe I can help convince him."

The front door opened to reveal two men in their late twenties, Indy's friend, Deputy Roman Shark, and Liz's brother, Kale. Roman was a baby-faced deputy with more of a charismatic appeal than actual good looks. Kale was more of the rugged, outdoorsy type, despite the fact that his chosen profession was a mortician. Liz and Kale inherited the funeral home only a few miles from the Stryker homestead. Their uncle died unexpectedly, leaving them the family business. If it hadn't been for their relocation last year, Indy's father never would have met Liz. The cheerful holiday mood was interrupted by the two men, who were arguing as they entered with a tangled ball of outside lights.

"This wasn't my fault," Roman announced.

"Well, it certainly wasn't mine," Kale remarked. "I wasn't even around last Christmas."

"Fine, blame the commander, if you dare."

The comment was enough to stop Kale just a few feet into the foyer. "From what I've heard about Indy's father, I don't want to upset him," he suddenly announced.

Indy and Liz exchanged humored looks then glanced over the railing at the two men in the foyer below.

"What's the problem, boys?" Liz asked while cleverly raising her brow in question.

Roman indicated the massive, tangled ball of lights. "A little tangle in the lights."

Indy wasn't surprised. It had been five years since the lights had been used, and her father had carelessly torn them down the day after Christmas during a fit of rage. It was a long story. Indy doubted the lights would even work. Hopefully, between the two men, they would check that they were operational before going to the trouble of hanging them. A young, raven-haired woman the same age as Indy appeared from the kitchen carrying a tray of eggnog served in festive glasses. Margo Langley had been Indy's best friend from the time she started college five years ago. Although an attractive woman in her own rights, Margo projected a tough girl attitude. It was mostly an act to keep men at a distance. She had a bad breakup before Indy had met her and clearly wanted nothing to do with the entire male population.

"Who's up for a little holiday cheer?" Margo announced with giddy enthusiasm.

Judging by her excessive cheerfulness, she'd already sampled the eggnog several times to make sure it turned out correctly. Indy wasn't ruling out her friend being drunk.

"Is that Mrs. Stryker's recipe?" Roman eagerly asked, his eyes glued to the filled glasses.

"Yes, it's Indy's mother's recipe."

Roman practically tossed the tangled lights into Kale's arms and lunged for Margo holding the tray of eggnog. He grabbed a glass, sipped the thick milky contents, and groaned his delight.

"Oh, yeah, that's the stuff. I haven't had any of this since--" Roman suddenly hesitated, smiled with embarrassment, and took another sip.

Indy thought it was adorable how sensitive her friends were regarding her mother's death, but it wasn't necessary. She'd made her peace with her mother's tragic accident a long time ago.

"It's been five years since she died, Roman," Indy informed him. "You can speak of my mother."

Despite her reassurances, Roman didn't appear convinced and swiftly changed the topic.

"I'm so glad you're having this party. It's been too long," Roman announced then looked at Liz as she descended the stairs to retrieve her own glass of eggnog. "The Stryker Christmas parties were legendary. Half the town would show up."

"Don't forget my father's team," Indy announced cheerfully.

Indy strayed into her own fantasy. It felt like an eternity since her father's team was around for a lengthy visit. Everything seemed to fall apart after her mother's car accident. It was as if Indy had been abandoned by her only family when she needed them most. Of course, she had been away at college most of that time, which probably had something to do with how alone she'd felt back then. Thankfully, that was around the time she'd met Margo. Roman had been a good friend, but he lacked that certain seriousness Indy desperately needed. Margo liked to refer to Roman as their comic relief. Although Indy had graduated college last year, her father's team seemed to keep their distance. She couldn't deny that she missed them. It was almost heartbreaking.

"Can't forget about your father's team. They're the best part," Roman announced and jolted Indy back into reality. He released a throaty chuckle and seemed pleased. "It's not a party without your friendly neighborhood Delta Force."

Indy gently cleared her throat and gave Roman a stern look. Roman hid his embarrassed smile.

"Sorry," he remarked timidly and corrected himself. "Operational Detachment Troop."

"You seriously don't think anyone else knows they're Delta--?" Liz began but Indy quickly silenced her.

"Acht," Indy reprimanded Liz.

Liz seemed humored by Indy's lecturing and motherly instincts regarding her father and his team.

"I can't wait to get to know this unruly bunch," Liz said while smiling fondly. "I barely got to meet them the last time they were around, though Flynn talked about them all the time."

"I'll admit, I'm a little intimidated at the thought of four men in Special Forces grilling me about my relationship with Indy," Kale remarked.

Indy cast a look at him but didn't comment. She didn't feel like getting into another debate with him about their *non-existent* relationship. Kale hadn't met her father, despite his sister having dated Flynn for the five months prior to his last deployment. Although neither would admit it, Indy suspected Kale and Liz had some sort of falling-out when they first took over the funeral home. Liz was eager to move out the first chance she got.

"The commander is rather *impressive*," Margo informed Kale while holding back her grin.

"He most certainly is," Liz announced while smiling dreamily, unable to disguise her bedroom eyes. "I can't wait until he gets home."

"I guess no one in this house is sleeping for a few nights," Roman teased.

Liz playfully smacked Roman's arm.

"My father hasn't been home for Christmas since my mother died," Indy informed them then momentarily drifted into her own thoughts. She warded off her self-pity and returned to reality. "It was very painful for all of us. I think he's been avoiding coming home for the holidays because of that."

"Losing your mother on Christmas Eve--" Roman began, realized he's spoken aloud, and then immediately silenced.

Margo swiftly changed the subject to something less traumatic. "So, tell me about these hardcore men of his, and why I've never met them," she demanded.

"That's probably because you've only lived around here the last year since college graduation," Indy reminded her. "My father's team hasn't been around much this past year. Even Liz only met them that one time."

"Remind me which one is the womanizer, so I can avoid him," Margo remarked in a teasing tone, but Indy knew she was serious about avoiding him.

Liz sat on the bottom step and grinned while holding her glass of eggnog. She placed her chin in her hand and gave the appearance of an innocent schoolchild about to be told a story.

"Yes, tell us about Flynn's team," Liz announced. "I'd like to hear the real story on these guys. Flynn talks about them as if they're his golfing buddies."

Roman laughed at the comment. It would be very hard to imagine any of them in preppy golf attire. Everyone settled in for story hour and gave Indy their undivided attention. Like her father, she always told good stories. Unlike her father, she didn't embellish for the sake of drama. Despite telling everyone it was okay to discuss her mother, Indy was grateful for the change of subject. She didn't need thoughts of her mother's death overshadowing the happy occasion of her father's return after his five-month hiatus. Besides, she loved talking about the men in his team. They were her family since she was a little girl and a major part of her life growing up.

Chapter Two

The remote island, located several miles off the coast of Ecuador, was home to a massive compound with a small army protecting its infamous leader. Santiago Perez, self-proclaimed president of the island, secured his legacy as a businessman and friend to locals. To United States intelligence agencies, he was a drug lord, mass murderer, and terrorist. Santiago's compound was a hacienda style castle with two watchtowers, gatehouse, and tall walls meant to keep unwanted visitors out. Unfortunately, for Santiago, his unwanted visitors were already within the confines of his castle compound. The heavily armed, well-lit compound was alive with activity as men on walls fired shots into the acre-sized enclosure within the castle walls. Some appeared to be firing blindly, which wasn't surprising, since the elite team of Delta Force's combat squadron had them nearly shooting themselves.

An imposing, bald man in his mid-forties, Flynn Stryker, fired his assault rifle at the armed guards shooting in his general direction. He clenched a cigar between his teeth and had a hardened look on his face as he took out two guards before they even realized where the shooting originated.

"You've already met my father, the commander--" Indy began her narrative in a tone conveying childlike fascination. *"My father is*

tough but compassionate. He'd do just about anything to help someone in trouble."

An armed guard came around the corner behind Flynn. Flynn caught a glimpse of the guard. He tossed himself to the ground, rolled into a sitting position, and threw a knife into the man's throat. The guard collapsed, barely having time to clutch his bleeding neck as he fell to the ground.

"Then there's Nate Dax," Indy continued. *"He's a big, teddy bear."*

A large, massively muscular man, Nate Dax, held a dead guard against him as a human shield while firing at several guards. The dead guard took the brunt of the gunfire, his body jerking and jolting to the hefty gunfire.

"He just puts on a tough act. He's actually very sweet."

Once Nate had taken out the last of the guards firing at him, he casually tossed the blood-soaked, bullet-ridden man aside like a rag doll. The firing appeared to cease, finally ending the short-lived battle, although more men would soon be on their way.

" *Then there's Jackson North. You're going to love him,"* Indy announced. *"He's the sensitive, stylish one."*

A lanky, athletically built man, Jackson North, shoved a tied man with a black hood over his head to the ground near Flynn's feet. Jackson smiled charmingly and knocked the bound man over with his booted foot.

"Look who decided to join us," Jackson announced a little too proudly.

Flynn eyed the tied man on the ground and almost appeared surprised. "And he's in one piece," he remarked then grinned at Jackson. "I'm impressed."

"Don't be," Jackson retorted. "He won't be having children any time in the near future."

Flynn chuckled softly.

"Jackson is very charming and quite the ladies' man," Indy announced. *"Women find him irresistible."*

"He's probably going to think twice before jerking off as well," Jackson teased.

Nate glared at the lanky man and sneered his distaste for him. "What do women see in you?"

He immediately appeared offended while staring at his comrade. "I have a lovable personality."

"Speaking of lovable--" Flynn announced and looked around with great interest. "Where's our resident firebug?"

"He's finishing his shock and awe for our escape," Nate informed Flynn. "That boy enjoys his work a little too much."

"And then there's Harlan Temple, the warmest, sweetest man I know," Indy continued. *"He's like an uncle to me."*

Two guards appeared through a hidden doorway with their assault rifles aimed and ready for their attack on Flynn and his team. A man in his mid-thirties, Harlan Temple, appeared in the doorway behind the armed guards. He punched and kicked them in the knees and the face with amazing karate skills. He stabbed the first man in the throat, kicked the second in the abdomen, and pulled the knife from the first guard as he fell. Harlan flipped the knife through the air, kicked the second man again, caught the knife on its descent, and stabbed the second guard in the neck. He casually joined his team as if nothing had happened and smiled cheerfully.

"Did you see the roses in that garden back there?" Harlan asked while giving a general nod behind him and removed a delicate red rose from his pocket. He twirled and studied it reflectively. "Now *that* is beautiful."

Nate glared his disapproval and nearly dropped his assault rifle. "You stopped to pick flowers?"

"I just love him to death," Indy announced.

"I hardly stopped--" Harlan retorted, displaying his annoyance. He removed a remote control from his pocket and flashed it to his men. "Ready to blow this joint?"

Flynn grinned while appearing pleased and arrogantly cocked his head to the side. "On your mark."

Harlan smirked slyly. "Mark--" He pressed the remote control button.

The other three ducked with anticipation of the explosion while Harlan remained casually standing. Nothing happened. All four looked at the intact compound with shared confusion.

"What the hell--?" Flynn launched.

Harlan stared at the remote control and appeared stunned. "That's never happened to me before."

Jackson casually placed his hand on Harlan's shoulder, gave him a mocking sympathetic look, and patted him. "Happens to all men eventually."

Harlan pressed the button several times with increasing anxiety. Nothing happened. The sound of faint gunfire was heard behind them. Nate suddenly went down. The other three dived to the ground and took shelter behind a stone fountain. They looked around with surprise.

"The rest of his men are already here," Flynn cried out. "It's a trap! We were set up!"

Nate moved to his knees, returning fire despite his bleeding shoulder, and took cover with them behind the fountain. He looked pissed more than injured.

"In ten minutes, we're going to have fifty or more men to our rear waiting to shoot us in the ass!" Jackson announced boldly while shifting looks to Flynn as he fired back at the guards now flanking them.

"We're pinned," Flynn informed them and looked at his men. "Options?"

Nate, who practically ignored his injury, looked at Flynn with all seriousness and cast a glance at the bound, hooded man lying on the ground taking shelter from the gunfire.

"Use the prisoner as a human shield," Nate casually suggested.

"The explosives can be detonated manually," Harlan informed Flynn. "Small weapons fire--"

Flynn glared at Harlan with disapproval. "You'd have to be too close for that to work," he remarked expressing his annoyance. "That's a one-way trip. No one's going back in there."

Jackson took a shot to his upper arm. He moved the assault rifle to his left hand and resumed firing. Harlan looked from both injured men to Flynn and offered a tiny, knowing smile.

"Tell *my girl* I love her," Harlan announced. Without warning, he fired into the trees, popped up from the safety of the stone fountain, and ran for the compound, avoiding the barrage of bullets on his heels.

As he disappeared into the compound, Flynn could only watch with horror.

"That crazy son-of-a-bitch!"

Chapter Three

A guard stormed down the broad mansion staircase with his assault rifle locked and loaded. The sound of gunfire could be heard coming from the back castle grounds, which had alerted more guards to the location of the perimeter breach. The armed guard reached the bottom of the stairs and ran for the main, outer doors. As he passed the darkened sitting room doorway, he was struck in the face with the butt of an assault rifle. The guard didn't even have time to gasp as he dropped to the floor. Harlan caught the man's weapon before it could strike the floor, preventing it from making a loud and distinctive clatter. The last thing Harlan needed was more guards alerted to his presence within the mansion itself. He looked at the motionless man on the floor by his feet.

"Pardon me."

Harlan slung the guard's assault rifle over his shoulder, hurried past the fallen man, and headed up the broad, marble staircase, taking two steps at a time. The sound of guards thundering along the second floor hallway could be heard. Harlan slung his own rifle over his shoulder, leaped over the railing, and clung to it on the outer side just out of sight. Two guards hurried down the stairs, unaware of his presence. Harlan leaped back over the railing feet first and struck the first man, who flew into the second man, knocking him off his feet as well. Both men tumbled down the stairs, making more noise than acceptable. Harlan continued up the stairs in more of a hurry now. As he reached the top of the stairs, more men were heard thumping along the hallway. Harlan appeared annoyed by the continual setback, preventing him from keeping his date with the elusive bomb. He darted into a nearby bedroom. As three guards appeared, one paused by the partially open bedroom door that now swayed slightly, indicating someone might have entered. The guard assessed the situation, raised his assault rifle, and slowly pushed the door open. He silently entered the nearly dark room.

†

Within the back garden, not far from what should have been their exit, Flynn, Nate, and Jackson continued to fire at the guards entering through their escape route. The stone fountain offered them little shelter from the barrage of bullets now being fired at them. A bullet whizzed past Flynn, narrowly avoiding him, but found its way into Jackson. Jackson was thrown to the ground and writhed in agony. Flynn caught of glimpse of his man going down, but before he could even react, it was soon obvious Jackson wasn't the only man down. Nate lie motionless on the ground not far from Jackson, his condition unknown. Flynn fired into the back entrance with more conviction, obviously angered by his men being shot. A bullet penetrated his shoulder and another found his leg, taking him to the ground. His assault rifle flew from his hand and landed several feet away.

Flynn clutched his bleeding shoulder and took a moment to endure the excruciating pain. He reached for the pistol on his hip, grinding his teeth to the enormous pain surging through his body. Guards were heard approaching from the back entrance and more appeared from the west wing of the mansion. Flynn clutched his pistol close to his chest and remained perfectly still while listening to the guards' approach. It wouldn't be much of a last stand, but he would take the first man with him. As their footfalls and the clattering of their weapons were heard closing in, a tremendous explosion shook the compound and the very ground beneath Flynn. The entire west wing was torn apart and completely leveled to the ground. Flynn rolled onto his belly and shielded his head, awaiting the usual aftermath of falling debris. The sheer force of the explosion, along with stone from the wall, brutally tossed the standing men several yards through the air, leaving the entire courtyard filled with a large cloud of dust and debris. As the dust settled, the fountain remained standing within a pile of rubble. Alongside the fountain lie Flynn's motionless body beneath the ruins, blood soaking his chest and shoulder.

"This is going to be the best Christmas ever," Indy announced. *"I can't wait to see my father and the guys again."*

†

Indy stood in the Stryker house foyer with her friends and Liz while all five indulged in a second glass of eggnog. It was possibly the first Christmas since her mother died that it actually felt like Christmas to Indy. She leaned against the banister with her glass of eggnog and remained entertained by her own fantasies despite the comedian show being presented by Roman. The others were laughing at him and having a good time. The strong eggnog may have been helping.

"I remember this one Christmas party where the commander got so drunk--" Roman began and was cut short by the ringing foyer phone.

Indy hurried past him to the phone on the nearby hall table. She picked up the cordless phone and tried to contain her overly enthusiastic good mood.

"Striker residence," she announced into the phone. Indy listened to the voice on the other end and responded, "Yes, this is Indy Stryker."

Indy hesitated as she listened to the voice on the other end. Horror swept over her. She could feel her legs turn weak as all blood drained from her face. Her glass of eggnog slipped from her hand and shattered on the floor. The others jumped with surprise, fell silent, and stared at Indy on the phone.

"What?" she suddenly gasped and fought her tears. "Is he okay?"

The four stared at Indy in concerned anticipation to the phone conversation. Indy gasped and placed her hand to her mouth while fighting her tears. Roman hurried to her side and took the phone from her. Liz grabbed Indy around the shoulder and waist before she could collapse to the floor. The tears streaking her face were enough to cause panic among those within the room while Roman talked to the person on the phone. Liz clung to Indy, keeping her from falling, and stared at her with alarm.

"Indy, what is it?" Liz gasped. The fear on her face conveyed that she already knew the answer.

Indy suddenly sobbed and could barely get the words out. "Dad and his team--!"

Chapter Four

The cargo freighter, Mourning Liza, had seen better days. How the old, rusted vessel stayed afloat in the calm waters just off the coast of Panama was a mystery. Several weary looking crewmen in tattered clothing and scruffy beards meandered along the severely out-of-date deck. The sound of an approaching helicopter caught their attention, causing all five men to stop what they pretended to be doing and watch the sky. The military helicopter soon came into view as it approached, heading directly for the floating junkyard of a ship.

Within the back of the helicopter, Liz and Indy looked at the ship in the near distance. Both stared with surprise at the sight as they approached.

"You've got to be kidding," Liz scoffed. "They're onboard *that* monstrosity?"

"Just stay calm and play nice," Indy informed her. "We don't want to upset the natives."

The helicopter lowered onto a small clearing on deck. Liz appeared apprehensive as the pilot shut down the helicopter and cast a glance at him.

"Maybe we should keep the chopper running," Liz remarked to the pilot.

He didn't respond. Indy opened the back door and climbed out, forcing Liz to follow, although she was in less of a hurry as the ambitious, young woman. The five scruffy crewmen eyed the two women with hard to read expressions. Liz grabbed Indy's arm while staring back at the frightening men.

"My God," she gasped softly. "They're going to marinade and roast us."

"Doubtful," Indy replied with little emotion and lacked Liz's concern for their situation.

Liz suddenly gasped and squeezed Indy's arm to the point of physically hurting her. "You mean they intend to use us as sex toys?"

Before Indy could respond to Liz's comment, several men dressed in black combat gear appeared from all ends with assault rifles aimed at them. Liz screamed and ducked behind Indy. Indy didn't even twitch.

"I'm Indy Stryker," she announced in a firm, authoritative tone. "I demand to see my father!"

The armed men lowered their weapons simultaneously, and the man in charge approached.

"Miss Stryker, sorry about the unwelcoming greeting," he announced. "We only just learned of you arrival an hour ago. We had to confirm it was you. You understand."

"Of course," she replied and released a shaken breath. "Please, just take me to my father."

"This way," he announced and extended his hand toward the rickety, rusted door.

Liz clung to Indy's arm as they crossed the deck toward the doorway. As they passed the downtrodden seamen, it became obvious they were much younger men in disguise. Although Indy had a good idea of what to expect arriving on the cleverly disguised military ship, she couldn't deny its impressive cover story. As they entered the ship's interior, it became apparent that the ship was well maintained and probably no more than a few years old. The further they descended into the ship's interior, the more sophisticated the technology became. They passed two armed guards standing before the open infirmary door. A man clearly of South American descent lie on a padded exam table with his wrists cuffed to either side, and his ankles were chained to the lower end. The man was in his forties and appeared visually regal, possibly a man of great wealth. Liz glanced into the room and stared at the man with surprise, possibly due to his restrained condition.

"Who's that?" Liz suddenly muttered to Indy, although loud enough to catch the guard's attention.

One of the guards closed the door without response. Indy didn't even take notice to the man within the infirmary.

"That's classified," the soldier leading them announced, void of emotion.

They approached a room just down the corridor. The soldier opened the door and stood aside, allowing them to enter. Flynn lie in his hospital bed with tubes in his arm and monitors surrounding him. Indy and Liz entered the room and stared with shared concern. Flynn slowly opened his eyes and smiled warmly. Indy ran to his bedside and hugged him while sobbing. He held her and managed a tiny grin.

"Now stop that. I'm far from dead."

Indy pulled away and attempted to control her emotions, allowing Liz the opportunity to hug and kiss him as well. Flynn stared at them.

"How on earth did you two find us?" Flynn asked with an expression resembling humor.

"You have no shortage of military friends willing to divulge sensitive, classified information to your daughter," Indy announced while wiping her tears.

"You didn't have to fly all the way out here," he informed both women. "I'm fine, really."

"What happened, Dad?" she asked gently.

Flynn casually shrugged then groaned, regretting the action by the pain it seemed to cause him. "We overstayed our welcome, that's all."

"That's all?" Liz suddenly erupted.

He looked at the attractive woman and smiled gently. "I'd rather not give details. It just upsets Indy."

"What about the guys?" Indy asked while sniffing and wiping her tears with trembling hands. "Are they okay?"

Flynn stared at her a moment then quickly attempted to cover for his strange look, but his shattered expression told a different, chilling story.

"Jackson and Nate are their usual, charming selves," he informed her while trying to sound positive. "They'll have a few new scars to tell wildly inaccurate stories about."

Indy knew something was wrong and stared at her father with concern. "What about Harlan?"

Flynn appeared uncomfortable and avoided looking at her. For a moment, he appeared to choke up. Indy felt her heart sink in her chest as her entire body twitched.

"Daddy, what about Harlan?" she gasped softly.

Flynn still didn't look at her and held back his sobs. Seeing tears come to her hardened father's eyes was almost unbearable. She'd only seen him cry once--when her mother died.

"They, uh, they don't think he's going to make it," he announced, his voice cracking. "He's, uh, in a coma."

Indy's expression shattered to the news. "No--"

A thousand memories of Harlan rushed through her subconscious. He'd been a major part of her life for as long as she could remember. The news was at best devastating. Liz clung to Flynn's hand and attempted to comfort him. Indy held back her tears, but it wasn't easy.

"What, uh, what happened?" Indy asked.

"We were ambushed," Flynn replied softly. "They somehow blocked the signal to his explosives, so the stupid bastard went back inside to manually detonate it. He had to get close enough for a small caliber bullet to hit it in exactly the right spot." The tears now flowed, and he was unable to stop them. "He gave his life to save ours."

Liz held Flynn, but he didn't respond well to being comforted in his emotional state. Liz took her cue and released him. He attempted a tough front but failed.

"We, uh, caught the remaining enemy by surprise when the compound blew and took them out," he announced in a quivering voice. "I went back for Harlan. He knew exactly where to position himself to avoid most of the blast, which kept him from going down with the building. He, uh, came to for only a second."

"Did he say anything?" Indy asked gently.

"He was disoriented," Flynn replied softly and sighed. "He just said 'Liz'."

Liz stared at Flynn with some surprise and nearly gasped. "He said my name?"

"I told you, he was disoriented."

Indy could barely control her trembling body. "Will they let me see him?" she asked gently.

"I don't think so, honey," Flynn replied softly. "He's in pretty bad shape. He's been in a coma since we pulled him out. If he stabilizes, they'll send him back to the states with us." Flynn then looked at Liz. “The guys and I decided we're going to stay as long as possible to be with him. I hope you understand.”

“Yes, of course,” Liz replied while clutching his hand then looked back at Indy. “We understand, don't--?”

Indy was gone.

Chapter Five

The male medic left the room marked ICU. Before the door even closed, Indy slipped into the room and quietly shut the door behind her. She looked across the room and saw what appeared to be Harlan in the hospital bed with tubes, monitors, and a respirator. His head was wrapped and both his lower arms and his left leg were in casts. Several scrapes and burns could be seen on what little parts of his body that remained exposed. Indy stared in horror at the man she once knew. She held back her sobs and slowly approached his bed. He didn't look like the man she remembered. He looked frail and only a shell of his former self. She touched his fingers that were sticking out from beyond the cast and stared at his scraped, bruised, and slightly scorched face. Indy held back her sobs, touched his face, and gently kissed the small portion of his forehead without bandages on it.

"Please don't leave, Harlan," she whispered softly with a quiver in her voice. "It'll kill the commander--and me too. I love you." She drew a deep breath while staring at him. "I just don't want to never have said that."

The door was heard opening, startling her. She knew she was going to be in trouble for secretly entering ICU. Indy sniffed and wiped her tears. It was going to take a lot of strength to contain her anger at the medic once he started yelling at her.

"You're not supposed to be in here," a familiar male voice announced.

Indy quickly turned and saw Jackson standing in the doorway in his hospital gown and robe. Indy hurried to him, no longer able to control her sobs and hugged him with the promise of never letting go. Jackson gingerly clung to her. He was obviously in a lot of pain, but he didn't share his discomfort. Indy pulled back just far enough to look into his eyes.

"How are you feeling?" she asked gently and quickly looked over him. "Are you okay?"

He smiled warmly and gently brushed the hair from her tear-streaked face. "I'm a lot better now that I've seen you."

Indy clung to him, buried her face into his shoulder, and managed a soft laugh. "You need a new line."

He snorted a soft laugh while holding her. "Uh, how about saving the sediments for when I'm wearing pants--and possibly underwear."

Indy pulled away, stared at him with surprise, and then playfully smacked him. He yelped with some discomfort. He gingerly rubbed the spot where she'd slapped him on his injured arm.

"That's still a little sore," he gently informed her. His timid smile immediately returned. "Why don't you go say 'hi' to the big guy? I'm going to say 'hey' to Harlan before someone throws me out."

Indy slowly nodded and again wiped her tears. She sniffed softly and stared at Jackson. "My father didn't offer much hope," she said gently and gave a slight nod toward the bed. "He'll be okay, won't he?"

Jackson again pulled her into his arms and warmly clung to her. He managed a soft, insincere laugh. "You know Harlan. He's got nine lives. Besides--" Jackson pulled back and looked into her eyes. "You know he's not passing up the opportunity to brag about how he saved our lives by blowing himself up. He's going to hold that over us the rest of his miserable life, I promise."

Indy managed a soft laugh, even if she didn't believe Jackson. The tears in his eyes were a dead giveaway that he was lying to make her feel better. Jackson grinned and firmly nodded her from the room.

"Go on," he announced. "Go see Nate. He's pretty cranky right now. Seeing you should cheer him up."

"He's a bad patient, I know."

"Considering he took a bullet to the ass, yeah, he's a bad patient," Jackson replied. "He took one look at the male medic and nearly jumped out of his bed."

"Not the suppository story again," Indy groaned.

"Yeah," Jackson replied with a sigh. "He never quite recovered from that little adventure."

"I won't bring it up, I promise."

Jackson appeared offended. "You're no fun."

Chapter Six

One week later. There was a buzz of excitement in the air as Indy thundered down the backstairs leading into the massive, modern kitchen. She nearly collided with Liz, who had been approaching the island counter with her morning coffee. Liz jumped with surprise, spilling coffee onto her satin robe. The grin on Indy's face was enough to make Liz forget about the spilled coffee as her eyes lit up with enthusiasm.

"Was that the call?" Liz nearly gasped.

Indy grinned and nodded. She was too excited to speak. "Harlan's condition stabilized," Indy managed to blurt out the words in rushed speech.

"He's out of the coma?" Liz asked with surprise.

"No, he's still in the coma," Indy replied but didn't allow that to distract from what was important. "They've cleared Harlan for transport. My father and his team are on their way home. They're already in the air."

Liz cried out excitedly, nearly threw her cup to the counter, and hugged Indy. Indy's cries of joy matched those of Liz. They hugged in an embrace that seemed to last forever. Liz suddenly pulled away and felt her hair. She looked at Indy with concern.

"How long until they get here?" Liz asked. "I have so much to do."

"Jackson and my father are accompanying Harlan and Nate to Durham VA Medical Center," Indy informed her. "Nate needs more surgery to his shoulder, so he'll have to stay a few nights. I said we'd meet them there, but Dad said we should just stay here. Once Nate is settled into his room, and they make sure Harlan is stable, they'll come back here." Indy glanced at the kitchen clock on the wall. "They should be here in a couple of hours."

Liz took a quick sip of coffee, cast her cup back onto the counter, and hurried for the backstairs. Indy understood that Liz would want to look her best for Flynn when he returned, which would require excessive primping on her behalf. After she thought about it, Indy realized it wasn't such a bad idea and ran up the steps after her.

†

The taxi pulled up to the Stryker house early that evening. The house was lavishly decorated with white and blue icicle Christmas lights hanging from both the first and second stories. White and colored lights alternated on the bushes in the front yard, and two large holiday wreaths hung from the main, double doors. Flynn and Jackson got out of the taxi with added soreness from their still healing injuries and the long flight from the military freighter where they had been recovering. Jackson joined the driver by the trunk to receive their duffle bags while Flynn stood alongside the taxi and stared at his decorated house. A tiny smile crossed his face, but there appeared to be something more lurking behind it. The front door opened to reveal Indy and Liz. Both hurried from the house to greet Flynn. Each woman hugged him with enthusiasm and excitement to his return. Flynn returned their warm embraces then recovered his military bag from Jackson. He placed his arm around Liz and allowed her to escort him into the house. Indy exchanged hugs and a quick, friendly kiss on the lips with Jackson before heading toward the house with him.

"How's Harlan?" Indy asked as they headed up the few steps to the porch.

Jackson placed his free arm around Indy's shoulder and held her to his side with affection. "He's, well, stable," he reported. "Nate's stuck at the hospital for a few days, so he's going to keep him company."

Indy stopped Jackson before the open door to the house and turned to face him. She stared into his eyes. Her look was serious and demanding.

"But *how* is he?"

Jackson inhaled deeply, avoided looking at her, and stared off a moment as if searching for the answer she wanted to hear. He finally met her gaze and offered a pleasant smile.

"He's still in the coma, but he's stable," he reaffirmed. "You can visit with him tomorrow, but I think it's best to avoid the topic anymore tonight. Your father really needs a stress-free night to unwind at home. I think he blames himself for Harlan's act of idiotic heroism."

She nodded in agreement. "Yes, you're right." Indy attempted a smile. "We'll have a wonderful evening, and then let the lovebirds have some privacy."

Jackson hugged Indy while chuckling softly. "You'd make an excellent military wife."

Indy groaned and pushed him away. She hid her smile. "I hope that wasn't a lame attempt to secure your own 'welcome home' romp."

"Be serious, Indy," Jackson retorted. "If I intended to make a pass at you, your head would be spinning with ecstasy, and you'd fall helpless to my power of seduction."

She eyed him then smirked. "Wow, someone's ego is still intact. Your 'power of seduction' never worked in the past," Indy announced. "I think I'm safe."

"That's cold," Jackson announced with a pouting look on his face.

Indy grinned, pleased with herself, and headed inside. Jackson reluctantly followed her, shutting the door behind him. As they entered the foyer, Flynn stood at the base of the stairs and stared silently at the ivy and bows cascading down the staircase from the second floor. Liz had mysteriously disappeared, possibly to get him a drink while he settled in. Jackson cast a look at his motionless commander without comment, picked up Flynn's bag, and took both upstairs. Indy paused alongside her father as he stared at the Christmas decorations.

"Do you like the decorations?" Indy asked cheerfully. "I tried to keep them exactly the way mom used to do them."

Flynn snapped out of his trance, looked at his daughter standing alongside him, and smiled warmly. "Yes, everything is perfect, darling."

He pulled her into his arms and held her as if he'd never let go. Indy returned the embrace, although, she couldn't help feeling that something was wrong. Was he displeased about the decorations? Had he been suffering in silence about what happened at the compound? She knew about PTSD and realized she'd need to keep an eye on her father's moods for a while. Hopefully, after a few days at home, he'd be feeling his old self. Until then, she'd offer as much support as possible. Thankfully, Jackson and Nate would be staying with them for a few weeks. The more friends he had around to support him, the faster he'd bounce back from whatever had happened at the compound. Liz appeared in the foyer with the familiar silver tray and four, festive glasses of eggnog. Flynn released Indy, offered Liz a grateful smile, and accepted a glass of holiday cheer. Indy saw his hand trembling as he picked up the glass. Concern rippled through her body, but she attempted to keep it buried inside for now. Her father needed a night of normalcy and, perhaps, a few more glasses of eggnog.

Chapter Seven

It was two days later and nearing evening. The Durham VA Medical Center in North Carolina was a ten-story modern marvel of brick and mason. The 274-bed facility housed military men and women either recovering from recent injuries returning from active duty or those requiring medical attention in the years following their discharge. The patient's rooms, although clearly sterile and reminisce of a hospital, had a slightly homey feel for the comfort of their honored, recovering guests. Harlan lie in his hospital bed beneath the sterile, white sheets. He was still attached to tubes and monitors while remaining in his comatose state. The respirator had been removed and the injuries to his face appeared to be healing. Indy sat in a comfortable chair facing him and held his fingers, which stuck out beyond his cast. A book lie open on her lap as she softly read to him. A cheerful yet sophisticated looking doctor in his late forties, Dr. Perry, entered the room while scanning through Harlan's chart. When she stopped reading, Dr. Perry looked at Indy, who was now silent while watching him. He managed a tiny smile and almost appeared embarrassed.

"I didn't mean to interrupt story time."

She would have to admit, she didn't feel comfortable reading in front of others, but she was more interested in any new findings from the distinguished looking doctor.

"I have all evening," Indy replied while studying him. "How is he?"

Dr. Perry finished skimming the chart and looked back at her with a more pleasant smile. "Apart from the obvious, he's physically healing," he informed her. "There's no internal damage, and we're fairly confident there's little to no brain damage. His body is just in a state of shutdown while trying to heal itself." He briefly glanced at the chart and raised his brows with what he read. "Apparently his brain played ping-pong inside his skull." He looked up at her. "He's lucky to be in such good shape."

"He's a war hero," she proudly informed him.

The doctor smiled in response. "So I've heard from the others who come to sit with him. I've seen devotion among those who serve, but Harlan seems to have more than earned respect from his team."

"They've served a long time together," she informed him. Indy felt uncomfortable, but she needed to be direct, since the medical staff had a way of dancing around the tough questions. "Do you think he'll come out of it?"

"I hear he's a tough one, so I'm going to say he has a great sporting chance."

She felt relief sweep over her, possibly for the first time. The fact that he didn't even hesitate before responding made her feel better than she had.

"Thanks, Doctor."

Dr. Perry checked a few of the monitors before leaving the room. Indy stared at the door after he was gone and sank into her own thoughts and concerns. There was little point to worrying herself over something she couldn't control. She shut the book, removed a comb from the drawer, stood over Harlan's bed, and styled his hair the way he usually wore it. She didn't like when the nurses gave him that flat back, college professor type hairstyle. He wore his neatly trimmed hair slightly spiky. She always thought it made him look somewhat unpredictable yet slightly cuddly. She heard of Harlan's reputation among the team with the stories they'd tell. She found most of them difficult to believe. Harlan had always been sweet and docile, in her opinion. She'd never seen him in action, but she never understood how anyone could fear such a sweet, caring man.

If she were honest with herself, he was her first childhood crush. He reminded her a little of her father, and most girls wanted a man like their father when they were little. It was those father like characteristics that later ended her crush. There was a time in a young woman's life when she wanted a man completely the opposite of her father. That's when she developed a slight crush on Jackson. Jackson, very much a lady's man, easily proved to her that he wasn't the type of guy she was looking for. By the time she was fifteen, she reserved herself to the fact that she did want someone like her father, and she was no longer ashamed to admit it. She even toyed with the thought that she'd someday marry Harlan, a typical teenage scenario. She never told anyone, but she cried when he met Maureen nearly seven years ago. She cried even harder when they were married the following year.

As Indy sank back into her childhood memories of Harlan and how much he'd been a part of her life, an attractive, dark-haired woman in her early thirties entered the room and stopped to watch Indy taking great care to style his hair. Maureen Temple smiled at the sight then finally approached the bed.

"Hey, Indy," Maureen said in a warm but soft tone, so as not to startle her.

Indy quickly turned, saw Harlan's wife, and held back her sobs. She took two steps toward her and gave her a warm embrace. Maureen returned the heartfelt hug.

"I was hoping to run into you," Indy announced while fighting her tears. She pulled away and smiled warmly at Maureen. "We kept missing each other the last couple of days."

"I've been working a lot of crazy hours."

Indy quickly stepped aside and offered Maureen the chair at Harlan's bedside. The attractive woman hesitated and seemed unusually uncomfortable.

"No, I can't stay long," she informed Indy. "I just wanted to see how he was doing today."

Indy couldn't help feeling a strange pang in the pit of her stomach. How could she drop by and not want to spend time with Harlan? She was his wife. He'd take comfort in knowing she was at his bedside...where she belonged. Indy brushed her feelings aside and attempted not to judge her.

"Dr. Perry is hopeful," Indy announced and again pressed the issue. "Why don't I leave you two alone for a few? I'll get us some coffee before they close the cafeteria."

Before Indy could make an attempt to slip from the room, Maureen responded, catching her attention.

"No, that's okay. Don't leave on my account," Maureen announced and smiled in a way that left Indy feeling confused. "I'm sure he'd rather have you read to him then hear about my crazy day at work."

She attempted to understand Maureen's reluctance to stay, and wondered if Maureen was somehow bothered by all the time she'd been spending with her husband. Indy again attempted to assure Maureen that it was better if she stayed with Harlan.

"It's more the sound of our voices than what we're actually saying," Indy announced while forcing herself to smile. She didn't know why she had to convince his wife to stay with him in his time of need. "I'm hoping hearing a familiar voice will help him find his way back." Indy decided she wasn't going to take 'no' for an answer and transformed into her father right before Maureen's eyes. "I'll give you two some privacy." She left the room, leaving Maureen with Harlan and their much-needed privacy.

Chapter Eight

The hospital cafeteria was starting to thin out after the busy dinner hour had ended. Those remaining were mostly visitors and the inpatients they were visiting. Indy paid for her cup of tea and sat at the first available table with her back to the wall. Perhaps her father had taught her to be slightly paranoid over the years. He preferred sitting with his back to the wall so he could watch those coming and going with the added bonus of not allowing anyone the opportunity to sneak up behind him. Was he paranoid? Perhaps, but with his profession, paranoia helped keep a man alive. Indy despised hospitals, although she doubted anyone really enjoyed being in one, whether visiting or staying. Her last visit to a hospital was the fateful Christmas Eve her mother had died. Indy made it to the hospital just in time to see the shattered look on her father's face and witness him crying for the first time, that she was aware. She never had a chance to say goodbye to her mother. Her thoughts again strayed to Harlan. She didn't need another tragic hospital tale to reinforce her dislike for them.

She immediately snapped out of her own thoughts when she saw Nate at the register with a cup of coffee. She wasn't sure he'd seen her, but he approached her table immediately after paying and joined her. He had a habit of appearing oblivious to things around him, but he knew what was going on more than people gave him credit. Nate had been unfortunate enough to require additional surgery after the compound assault. The man had more titanium pins in his bones than she could even recall. He was literally the man of steel. His additional surgeries required he spend extra time at the hospital once they returned stateside. Nate was a man who hated hospitals more than anyone else Indy had ever known. He firmly believed nurses were all out to stick things in his classified posterior, making him the worst patient of them all. Indy couldn't be sure, but she had a sneaking suspicion someone, who shall remain anonymous, had pulled a prank on the big guy, which led to the suppository paranoia. She'd never say the words aloud in fear Nate would kill the offending comrade. She liked Jackson and didn't want to see the big guy kill him.

"I thought you were in Harlan's room," Nate announced in his usual, emotionless manner.

Nate was a hard man to read, since he had a tendency to come across as cold and unfeeling, but he wasn't nearly as uncaring as most thought.

"Harlan and I were going to watch a football game tonight," he bluntly informed her while casually leaning back in his chair and taking up more room than two men. "You're throwing my entire schedule off."

She was certain Nate was bored to tears, being stranded in the hospital after his surgery yesterday. He certainly wasn't one to take it easy or let a little pain slow him down.

"Maureen came to visit, so I decided to give them a little privacy," Indy casually informed him, having to keep from sounding bitter about what happened just a few minutes earlier in Harlan's room.

"Maureen?" Nate inquired and appeared puzzled. "I poked my head into Harlan's room before coming down here. Maureen wasn't there."

Indy stared at Nate a moment and could almost feel her blood pressure rising. Did Harlan's wife just stop by to see if he still had a pulse? She wanted to tell herself it was none of her business, but she couldn't help feeling hostility toward the woman. If any of the guys felt the same about Maureen, none said anything to her about it.

Although, she doubted they would. It was a private boy's club, and they didn't openly share.

"I guess she needed to get home," Indy replied and immediately drank her tea to keep from commenting further.

She took a large swallow of tea and regretted it, burning her mouth on the steaming liquid. At least the hot sting took her mind off her secret contempt for Harlan's wife.

"Yeah, I guess," Nate muttered.

Judging by his tone, he may have been thinking the same thing, but Indy wasn't going to press him to gossip. Nate wasn't much of a talker, and he didn't subscribe to gossip. She'd need to go to Jackson for that sort of information.

"How long are they making you stay?" Indy asked instead, wanting to change the subject.

"I'm being discharged tomorrow morning," he interjected a little too quickly.

"Really?" she announced with some surprise. "I thought they'd keep you a few days."

"I'm sure they think they are too," he remarked, "but I'm being discharged tomorrow. My orders."

She should have realized as much. Nate would get his way, and the doctor's would give in to his heavy fisted tactics. He could be persuasive--and just a little intimidating.

"If you plan to stay at our place, I could take you home with me after my morning visit," she announced.

Nate eyed her and raised his brow in silent suggestion. Indy shifted in her chair. He had other ideas, and she was easily able to read his look.

"Or you could borrow my car," she muttered, giving in to the silent intimidation. "I'm sure my father or Jackson will stop by sometime in the afternoon."

"Yeah, I'd appreciate that," he announced and acted as if it was her idea. "It's like you read my mind."

Yeah, she read his mind all right. It was always a joy talking to Nate. He was the impossible older brother she never wanted. He'd been tormenting her from the day they'd met almost twelve years ago. Supposedly, he currently had a semi-steady girlfriend, who would be stopping by to spend the holidays. Indy couldn't wait to meet the woman who could tolerate Nate in large, sporadic doses. At least she wasn't some girl he'd just met the night before, which was his usual taste in women. Indy was proud to admit that she'd never had a crush on Nate.

†

It was less than an hour later, and Indy once again sat alone at Harlan's bedside. Soon Nate would be arriving to watch football with his comrade, and she would return home, knowing he had someone to watch over him for a few more hours. She again held Harlan's fingers. The open book set on her lap, but she had little enthusiasm for reading any more tonight. She'd finally gotten over her hostility toward Maureen, who'd made her obligatory two-minute appearance. Indy tried to focus on reading the book, which was nearly putting her to sleep. She dreaded turning the page and wondered if she could skip the rest of the chapter. It wasn't as if Harlan would remember her reading to him once he was out of the coma. She stared blankly at the page and desperately wished the book would spontaneously combust. She groaned softly and finally gave up, shutting the book.

"I have to be honest with you, Harlan, your taste in books is bizarre," she remarked with a dreary sigh and cast a glance at the unconscious man. "Tomorrow, I'm bringing in a steamy love story with explicit sex scenes. At least I won't fall asleep reading that to you."

Harlan's fingers gently moved within her hand. Indy stared at him with surprise and slowly stood. She clung to his fingers and watched him as her heart raced. Had she actually felt his fingers move or was it a spasm? His eyes were still closed, but she swore he'd given her a signal.

"Harlan?"

There was no response or reaction. Her heart sank, but she wasn't giving up just yet. Indy clung to his fingers and gently touched his face while leaning over him.

"Harlan?" she announced with firmness and slightly louder than necessary.

Harlan's fingers again moved against her hand and his eyes opened only briefly. Indy felt her entire body jerk with enthusiasm. Despite that he didn't make eye contact, she accepted his eye movement for the wonderful sign that it was. She fought her tears and clung to his hand.

"Harlan? Can you hear me?" she nearly gasped while starting at him.

There was no response. Indy felt her heart continue to pound in her chest. She couldn't let this moment pass. She needed to find some way to pull him out of his long sleep and bring him back to her.

"Please, say something," she nearly begged.

His lips parted as he softly exhaled. "Liz--" Harlan gasped softly.

Indy stared at him and appeared baffled by his choice of first words. Despite his rambling, she remained cheerful that he had taken the first step toward consciousness. She quickly kissed his forehead, nearly curled onto the bed alongside him, and hugged his neck as tears of joy streaked her face. Indy knew she should alert the staff of his semi-alert status, but she wanted to hold him a moment longer, allowing her tears to flow uninterrupted.

Chapter Nine

Four days later. An extremely alert Harlan sat up in his hospital bed and played with the bed remote. He simulated sounds, almost as if he were drunk, as the head of the bed raised and lowered. Flynn and Jackson stood at the foot end sharing the same, broad stance. Both had their arms folded across their chests and their chins against their fists as they silently observed their alert yet demented comrade. Their shared expressions conveyed their concerns even though Dr. Perry appeared pleased with Harlan's progress. The doctor flipped through Harlan's chart and smiled his approval at Harlan's childlike behavior.

"Apart from some swelling in his brain, he's physically fine," Dr. Perry announced cheerfully.

The doctor caught the unchanged expressions on the hardened faces of the silent men. Dr. Perry immediately fidgeted and allowed a tiny, nervous smile to escape and answered the men's silent question.

"We, uh, have him loaded up on pain killers," the doctor informed them.

Flynn watched Harlan intently, lifted his head, and appeared concerned. "I should certainly hope so," he finally muttered. "He's not usually *this* crazy."

The doctor studied both men a moment and appeared to hesitate before speaking. He gently cleared his throat. "At this point in time, he has no memory," Dr. Perry gently informed them and awaited their reaction.

Jackson and Flynn looked at the doctor and appeared surprised as their arms simultaneously fell to their sides.

"None?" Jackson suddenly asked.

"Define 'no memory'," Flynn growled in response.

"He doesn't know who he is, who you are, or the time of day," Dr. Perry informed them. "He does, however, know how to function and feed himself." There was a brief pause. The doctor seemed uncomfortable by the way the two men stared at him. "Could be a combination of pain killers, swelling of the brain, and emotional trauma," the doctor replied. "We won't know what sort of damage we're looking at until we wean him off the pain meds. Only time will tell."

Jackson and Flynn continued to stare at the doctor with the same stone-like expressions on their faces.

The doctor drew a deep breath and placed Harlan's chart on the bedside table. "I told his wife it's probably in his best interest to return to some sort of home environment and have a visiting nurse care for him. Being in the hospital isn't the proper environment for his recovery."

Indy entered the room with an armful of red roses. Her exceptionally good mood radiated with each step. She observed Harlan playing with the bed remote and could barely contain her grin despite his childlike actions.

"Looks like someone's feeling their drugs," she announced cheerfully, unaware of the tension within the room.

Harlan stopped elevating the head of his bed, pressed the nurse's call button, and simulated the sound of an explosion. He grinned and laughed like a demented super villain. He looked to his right, saw Indy with the flowers, and could barely contain his childlike fascination.

"Those are beautiful flowers!"

Indy approached him with the roses. Harlan gently caressed the flowers and smelled them. As he caressed the rose's petal, he drifted out a moment. He jolted back into reality and looked at Indy holding the flowers. He grinned as he stared at her.

"You're pretty."

Indy smiled at the compliment and kissed him on the cheek. As she placed the flowers in the vase on his bedside, Harlan watched her and grinned. He then looked at Flynn and Jackson by the foot end of his bed.

"She's got a great ass."

Flynn and Jackson stared at him with disbelief as their mouths fell open. Indy immediately straightened with surprise and looked back at him. She'd never heard him talk like that and certainly never directed at her. Indy felt her cheeks redden, but she allowed the comment to slide. Harlan wasn't exactly himself, and she needed to remember that.

"We'll work on cutting back the happy pills," Dr. Perry announced, having felt the tension immediately rise. "I think he's a little too happy."

"Yeah, I should say so," Flynn muttered.

"I'm not sure I've ever seen him this *happy,*" Jackson remarked and cast a look at Indy.

Flynn shifted his attention to the doctor, releasing his irritation by Harlan's comment, and appeared curious. "So when is Maureen taking him home?"

Dr. Perry fidgeted and seemed reluctant to respond. "She's not."

Indy turned toward the doctor with a look of surprise that matched her father's look. "What?"

"I think she's feeling a little overwhelmed by his condition," Dr. Perry informed them. "He's going to require a lot of care, and she doesn't feel she can handle him."

"So what are you saying?" Flynn demanded, his arms again crossing his broad chest.

"We're looking into a private care home," he replied. "As soon as a bed becomes available--"

"A nursing home?" Jackson suddenly interjected.

"No, that's not what I meant," the doctor replied while fumbling for a better response. "He needs someplace with a homier feel but still plenty of attention."

Jackson turned to Flynn and raised his brows with little emotion. "Are you still hearing nursing home?"

"Yes, Jackson, I am," Flynn announced sternly without looking away from the doctor.

"No, absolutely not," Indy cried out then looked at her father. "I'm not working right now. I can take care of him. I want to take care of him, Dad."

"Yeah, me too," Flynn replied firmly. He cast a glare at the doctor and straightened proudly. "He's coming home with us. Get that visiting nurse."

"Are you sure? It's going to be a lot of work for the first few weeks," Dr. Perry informed them. "There's no telling what he's going to be like when he comes off the pain meds."

"The man saved our lives. He's my comrade and one of my best friends," Flynn announced firmly and placed his hands on his hips in his best superhero pose. "We don't leave our men behind."

Indy felt relief sweep through her. She sat on the edge of Harlan's bed and held his head to her shoulder. Harlan smirked deviously, nuzzled her shoulder with his face, and then looked at Flynn.

"I think she likes me," Harlan announced then peered down Indy's shirt at her cleavage.

Chapter Ten

By the time Flynn's car pulled up to the home, tastefully decked out with Christmas decorations and lights, it was already dark. While Indy and Liz had traveled to the ship to stay with the injured men, Roman, Margo, and Kale had finished decorating the house for their return. It was the first time in years the home had more than just a plain wreath on the front door. As Indy got out of the car, she couldn't help but admire the lights, despite having seen them several times over the last two weeks. The white icicle lights on the house and the colored lights on the surrounding trees were enough to mesmerize her. She was finally in the holiday spirit. Her father's unit was alive and well, and Harlan was on his way to recovering. It was the only present she ever wanted.

Jackson and Flynn got out of the car without even taking a second look at the lights and helped Harlan from the backseat and into a rented wheelchair. Despite not knowing what world he was in at the moment, he stared at the lights on the house and appeared awestruck as Indy had.

"Oh, pretty lights," he gasped while staring wide-eyed as they pushed his wheelchair toward the house.

Indy glanced at Harlan, momentarily distracted by the lights reflecting from his dark eyes, looking more like the Northern Star. His expression was priceless. No matter what she'd heard about Harlan's professional life, she knew he was a romantic at heart. He recognized beauty in things most people wouldn't see. It was in his transfixed gaze that she saw a glimmer of the man she knew and loved.

†

Nate greeted the military formation parade surrounding the returned war hero as he was wheeled along the grand foyer. Harlan looked from the holly and ivy cascading down the stairway railing from the second floor to the poinsettia plants along the foyer tables. The precession continued into the broad hallway along the family room. The fireplace toward the back of the family room was lavishly decorated with candles and Christmas decorations. Liz stepped out of the kitchen while drying her hands on a dishtowel and watched in silence. The look on her face was a complex mixture of curiosity and skepticism. She followed the precession down the hall and to the guest bedroom at the back of the house.

Despite being called a guestroom, the backroom was technically the same size as the second floor master bedroom. It had glass doors leading outside onto the sunset veranda, its own fireplace, a large, walk-in closet, and a private bath with a standing shower and deep garden tub. Even though it was dark outside, the room remained bright and cheerful. Several Christmas decorations had been hurriedly assembled in the room to make Harlan feel at home. The king-sized bed was overloaded with assorted colorful pillows and a plump comforter. The television was hidden within the expensive armoire across the room.

Jackson carelessly tossed the decorative pillows aside and pulled down the comforter. Nate and Flynn helped Harlan from the wheelchair to the bed. He managed to hobble on his casted leg while each held onto an elbow just above his arm casts. Liz paused alongside Indy in the doorway and watched the three, hard-core military men cater to their fallen comrade. It was a priceless moment. Jackson was quick to remove Harlan's shoe from his non-broken leg while Nate moved the wheelchair away from the bed. As

Flynn unbuttoned Harlan's jacket, he caught a look from the mildly battered man.

"I'd rather have the pretty lady undress me," Harlan announced and indicated Indy in the doorway.

Flynn straightened while allowing a low groan to escape. He smirked with all the charm of a rattlesnake and casually placed his hand on Harlan's shoulder. He hunched over slightly and looked directly into Harlan's eyes.

"I know you're not responsible for your actions, Harlan, so let me say this clear and slow for you," Flynn announced in what was meant to sound like a pleasant tone but failed. "That pretty girl is my daughter. You're like an uncle to her. If you so much as look at her wrong, I'm going to castrate you without a second thought. Are we clear?"

Harlan stared into Flynn's eyes only a few inches from his. He had a strange look in his nearly clueless eyes.

"Are you my father?"

Flynn groaned, rubbed Harlan's shoulder, and cast a look at Nate and Jackson.

"Get him changed into his P.J.'s," Flynn said with defeat then looked at Indy and Liz. His motion was quick and firm. "Ladies, out."

Indy and Liz were quick to leave the doorway and return to the hallway. Flynn entered the hallway and passed them while shaking his head. Liz and Indy filed in behind him. Indy knew her father was conflicted. His disgust was evident, yet he had nothing but respect for his best friend.

"Until he's off the Viagra-laced pain pills, I think you ladies need to avoid contact with him," Flynn gruffly announced.

Indy could tell from his expression that it hurt him even to say the words. Liz hurried alongside Flynn and kept stride with him. Her look was harder to read.

"Flynn, we really need to talk about this," Liz remarked with a tone of concern in her voice.

"I'm sorry, Liz," Flynn informed her while attempting to retreat from soldier mode and back into that of her boyfriend. "I should have talked to you first, but I couldn't let them put him in some home and hope they'd rehabilitate him." He cast a sympathetic glance at her. "I had to do this."

"I know, it's just a little heads up would have been nice," she replied.

"It's my fault," Indy quickly announced and hurried to keep up with them. She needed to protect her father's relationship. She didn't want to see him lonely again. "I insisted. I'm very persuasive."

Liz looked back at Indy and smiled timidly. "It's nice how you two stick up for each other."

Flynn stopped near the large bar that seemed to separate the kitchen from the family room. He grabbed the first bottle he found and filled a glass with the contents. Liz leaned on the bar near him and studied him in silence a moment as he drained the entire contents of the glass.

"I understand why you had to bring him here, I really do," Liz gently announced.

Indy studied her father's expression as he stared inside his empty glass. She was usually good at reading his expressions, but his current look was puzzling to her. She hoped he wasn't having second thoughts about allowing Harlan to recover at their house because Liz was moderately opposed to him staying.

"But--?" Flynn remarked softly without looking at her.

There was a long silence. Indy knew it was none of her business, and she wanted nothing more than her father to find happiness with Liz, but she was going to defend Harlan to the death, if necessary. Indy watched both with silent anticipation as her heart pounded harshly in her chest.

"There isn't one," Liz replied softly. "The man saved your life, so it's the least any of us can do."

Flynn's head suddenly lifted and his surprise was evident. He looked at Liz as if he had been prepared for a verbal assault, but when it didn't come, he was left speechless. A warm smile crossed his face.

"I appreciate that, Liz," Flynn replied and seemed to relax for the first time.

It was now Liz's turn to tense. "What about the party? Christmas Eve is in two days."

Flynn shifted slightly but assumed his commanding role. "Oh, Liz. I'm sorry," he announced while shaking his head. "We can't have all those people here. I canceled the invites." His look was sympathetic yet stern. "I hope you don't mind, it'll just be the guys and a couple of close friends."

Despite his sincere sounding, 'I hope you don't mind', his mind had already been made up on the matter. Liz seemed disappointed but hid it well. She knew better than to argue after all Flynn and his men had been through. Indy knew how disappointed her father's girlfriend must have felt, since she too would miss the grand party, but her father was right. Harlan needed time to recover and a big party wasn't the proper atmosphere. There would be other holidays to celebrate.

"I suppose that's best," Liz replied then collected herself. She looked at Indy and attempted a smile. "Indy, why don't you help me with dinner? You can make a tray for Harlan. You know what he likes."

Indy nodded and headed to the kitchen with Liz. She watched the woman in silence. She wished she could offer some verbal support, but they were on opposing teams at the moment. Liz would need time to warm up to the idea of Harlan staying long-term with them and the excessive care he would require. Liz had only gotten her slightly war-torn man back in her life after a five-month stint in God-knows-where. Indy knew Liz and her father hadn't had a great 'welcome home' celebration. Flynn's physical injuries paled in comparison to his emotional ones while dealing with Harlan's touch-and-go condition. He'd been emotionally distant during what little time he'd spent at home and around Liz. Indy just hoped the couple could survive the recent drama. She was fairly confident her father and Liz hadn't even been intimate since his return, which screamed trouble in her mind. Indy would have to work especially hard to keep her father and Liz from being torn apart.

Her father needed female companionship in his life, and he was lucky to find someone like Liz, who was willing to spend a great deal of time waiting for her man to return home. The thought of her father's sexual needs made her slightly nauseous. Something that delicate in nature required an expert on the subject of fornication. She'd need to call Jackson into duty.

Chapter Eleven

It was early the following morning, and Indy was almost certain she'd be the first person up. She hurried down the backstairs and entered the kitchen. To her surprise, Jackson was already comfortably seated at the island counter while sipping his morning coffee and reading the sports section of the newspaper. She couldn't understand how he could have gotten up before her. She hadn't heard him in the shower, being their bedrooms shared a bathroom. He looked shower fresh, so he'd obviously taken one. He glanced up and noticed her at the bottom of the stairs. Jackson smiled his usual, charming smile.

"Good morning," he announced cheerfully. "You're a late riser."

Indy wanted to smack Jackson. He didn't have to gloat or be so cheerful. His perfect existence irritated her.

"I thought I'd check on Harlan before having my morning tea," she announced and headed across the kitchen.

"The visiting nurse arrived," Jackson announced and returned his attention to the paper on the counter. "You may want to hold off on that impromptu visit. He may be indecent."

She stopped just past the island counter then turned to face him with a look of surprise on her face. "The visiting nurse is here this early?"

Jackson glanced at her with a dumbfounded look. "Early? Indy, it's nearly seven o'clock." He shook his head and turned his attention back to the paper. "College has made you soft."

Indy glared at the back of Jackson's head. If he saw the look she'd been giving him, he wouldn't be so smug. She loved the man, but she sometimes hated him with a passion. She'd forgotten how much Jackson annoyed her. Another older brother she never wanted. He glanced back at her, relished in her annoyance, and then finally grinned.

"What? No come back?" he remarked with a sinister smile that she wanted to wipe off his face.

He set his cup down and approached the stove on the opposite side of the island counter. He removed her favorite mug from the cupboard, placed a tea bag in it, and poured steaming water into the cup. He returned to the counter and set the mug on the corner near her. Jackson casually returned to his seat and slid the container of artificial sweetener toward her. She wanted to resist the urge to smile, but she loved the oaf too much. Indy joined him at the counter and added sweetener to her tea. Sometimes, having a surrogate big brother wasn't so bad. She then thought about last night and the tension between her father and Liz. She dunked her tea bag a moment in silence then glanced at Jackson. Despite his concentration on the newspaper, he acknowledged the look she didn't think he'd even seen.

"What's on your mind?"

"Should I be worried about my father?" she asked gently.

Jackson pushed the paper aside, turned on his chair to give her his full attention, and leaned his elbow on the counter, resting his temple to his fist.

"Why? Do you think he's behaving oddly?" Jackson asked while cleverly raising his brow.

She fidgeted slightly. Jackson had a tendency to psychoanalyze her at times, and he did it upfront just to annoy her.

"There seems to be a lot of tension between him and Liz," she replied.

"Tension?" Jackson questioned. "You mean with Harlan crashing the party?"

"No, there was tension before that," she replied.

"I haven't noticed any tension between them."

"They've been apart five months," Indy announced with a soft sigh. "He should be all over her."

"Monitoring your father's sexual habits?" Jackson raised his brows and grinned slyly. "That's pretty disturbing behavior, little girl."

"Don't call me that," she snapped hotly.

She hated when Jackson referred to her as a little girl. It was an insult, especially considering he'd tried to get her into bed on more than one occasion.

He inhaled deeply and straightened without taking his eyes off her. "Under normal circumstances, I'm sure they'd be going at it like rabbits on ecstasy," Jackson informed her, "but your father has a lot of his mind right now. Despite what you may think you know about men, sex isn't always the first thing on our mind. Always in the top ten; but not always the first thing."

"So you don't think there's a problem between them?" she asked and felt a moment of relief.

Jackson made a face and waved her off. "Nah," he replied without forethought. "Your father's a complex guy, despite what anyone says. He's just worried about Harlan. We all are." Jackson smiled more naturally. "But now that Harlan is somewhat alert, things are going to get better for all of us." He returned to his coffee, took a sip, and didn't bother looking back at her. "It'd be difficult for your father, night after night, to lie alongside that woman and not jump her."

She suddenly frowned. Now he was just annoying her for his own amusement. "Okay, more information than I needed," Indy muttered.

"You brought it up," he casually replied and hid his grin.

†

Liz slept peacefully beneath the covers on the king-sized bed within the master bedroom. Flynn stood before the long dresser and watched the sleeping woman through the mirror. His stare was fixated and almost sad. He looked at the carved box on top of the dresser, hesitated, and opened it. Setting on top was his white gold wedding band. He stared at it a long moment then picked it up and slipped it onto his left ring finger. He stared at the ring on his finger for the longest time in silence. Liz stirred and stretched beneath the covers. Flynn quickly removed the wedding band and returned it to the box. He looked over his shoulder at the woman lying in his bed. She was again asleep. Flynn ran his hand over his bald head, cursed softly under his breath, and headed for the bedroom door. He left the room, silently shutting the door behind him.

Chapter Twelve

A loud crash from the guest bedroom startled Indy and Jackson within the kitchen. Both sprang up from their pub chairs, hurried down the hall, and ran into the guestroom. An attractive nurse in her early thirties, dressed in a festive scrub uniform, darted across the room and away from Harlan's bedside. Harlan was sitting up in bed with his casted leg hanging over the edge. He threw a water glass at the nurse that nearly hit her in the head. The nurse, Callie, screamed as it shattered against the wall near the armoire. She hurried for them and immediately hid behind Jackson.

"He's crazy!" Callie screamed.

"She tried to kill me!" Harlan lashed out while pointing at her. He had a look in his eyes that was nearly frightening, reminding Indy of a mad dog.

"It's a sedative," the nurse protested to Harlan then looked at Jackson and Indy. "He became agitated."

"She was going to stick that thing up my ass," Harlan shouted back while struggling to get out of the bed and to his feet. His determination to get up was concerning.

Callie glared at Harlan from her position behind Jackson. “It's a suppository,” she launched back. “You haven't had a bowel movement in two days.”

“Don't you fucking worry about my bowels!”

Callie stepped alongside Jackson and glared at him. “Either he's sedated, or I won't take care of him.”

“If she comes near me again with that needle or that bullet, I'll snap her fucking neck!” Harlan shouted back, ready to jump from the bed, which would almost certainly land him on the floor.

Indy couldn’t believe the words coming from Harlan’s mouth. She’d never heard him threaten anyone, particularly a woman, and his tone was startling.

“That's it, I'm out of here!”

Callie grabbed her bag, stuffed her needles and suppositories into it, and stormed from the room. Indy and Jackson stared after her with surprise at what had just happened. Jackson suddenly turned and glared at Harlan.

“What the hell is wrong with you?” Jackson demanded.

“That fucking bitch tried to kill me!”

“Stop with that language,” Jackson yelled back and appeared ready to strike his friend.

Flynn hurried into the room, stared at the mess scattered on the floor, and then looked at the irate Harlan, who still attempted to get out of the bed. Liz, in her satin robe, arrived only a moment later.

“What the hell--?” Flynn demanded.

Jackson turned to face Flynn with a moderately concerned look. “He flipped out on the visiting nurse. She's gone.”

“Perfect,” Flynn groaned and scratched his bald head. He sank into thought for only a moment then motioned wildly. “Everyone out. He's my responsibility.”

“Dad, wait.”

Flynn spun to face Indy with a look of frustration she rarely saw. “I said out, Indy,” he announced firmly. “I don't want you anywhere near him right now.”

“Let me handle this,” Indy quickly informed him. “He's not going to hurt me.”

“You think you know that man?” Flynn demanded while pointing at the man struggling to climb out of the bed. “Well, you don't. Harlan’s in combat mode. He's liable to hurt you without even trying.”

“Dad, it's Harlan. Just give me a chance to calm him down,” she announced then turned sympathetic. “Please, trust me. Trust him.”

Flynn considered her comment a moment, appeared defeated, and then groaned softly while nodding. Flynn, Jackson, and Liz remained just inside the doorway. Both men kept close watch on their injured comrade. Indy approached Harlan, who struggled in vain to get out of bed. He glared at her as she got closer with an unpredictable, harsh look. It was almost enough to stop her approach, but she wasn't going to let him intimidate her. She summoned her courage and paused two feet before him.

"Do you need some help?" Indy asked gently.

Harlan's look immediately softened, and he appeared defeated. "I need to use the bathroom."

"I can help you."

Indy took a step closer to his bed and offered her arm to him. Harlan eyed her then took her arm and allowed her to help him stand. He limped on his casted leg while clinging to her arm with his arm in the cast. She assisted him to the guestroom's private bathroom. Indy spent an awkward moment helping him onto the toilet while attempting to keep from looking. She left the bathroom and gave him some privacy. When he announced he was finished, she helped him back to the bed. He appeared relaxed and calm after his bathroom visit. Flynn and Jackson cleaned the broken glass from the floor while closely watching Indy and Harlan.

"Would you like to get washed and dressed now?" Indy asked as he situated himself on the bed.

"You won't let that woman near me, will you?" he demanded as his temper rose slightly.

"No, she's gone."

His look was serious as he stared into her eyes. "She tried to kill me."

"She won't be back."

Harlan uncertainly looked at the casts on each of his arms then back at Indy as he exhaled with defeat. "I can't wash myself. Can you take these things off?"

"Your casts have to remain on for now," Indy replied gently. "I'll help you wash."

Flynn suddenly straightened and nearly dropped his dustpan filled with broken glass. "Indy--"

Indy could feel her father's eyes on her, but she refused to look back at him. She gave Harlan a serious look while indicating her father.

"Do you recognize that man?"

Harlan glanced past her to Flynn, who stared intently. He looked back at Indy. "He's mean," he announced in a soft tone. His eyes widened dramatically as he whispered, "He wants to castrate me."

"That's your commanding officer, remember?"

Harlan stared at her a moment with bewilderment then shook his head.

"He's my father, and he's very protective of me," she informed him in a stern tone. "If I help you wash and dress, you'll mind your hands, right?"

"Yes, I'll mind my hands," Harlan announced then studied her and smiled. "What's your name?"

"Indy, remember?"

Harlan again shook his head. The lost look in his eyes reinforced that he had no idea who she was.

"It'll come back to you, I promise."

Harlan's smile brightened. "I hope so," he replied. "I'd like to remember you."

Indy straightened while taking a deep breath then looked around the room. "Everyone out," she commanded.

"Indy, I'm not sure--" her father protested.

"I said out," she announced sternly. "I don't need the added embarrassment of an audience. Wait in the hall if you must, but close the door behind you."

She had successfully surprised both men with what was almost certainly a direct order. Oddly enough, both obeyed without further protest. A few minutes later, Indy had a washbasin alongside the bed. She sat on the bed facing Harlan with the covers up to his waist. He held a hand towel and dried his face while she washed his chest and shoulder. Indy tried desperately to clear her mind and pretend it wasn't Harlan she was bathing. As she washed his chest, her eyes strayed to every scar, which there were many, and some she'd never seen before. His body was a road map of the many coups in which he'd partaken. Each scar pained her. She'd never realized how much action he'd actually seen.

Not an outwardly muscular man like Nate, Harlan's lean body had hidden excessively toned arms, shoulders, and abs. It occurred to her that she'd never actually seen him without his shirt. Unlike Nate and Jackson, he wasn't nearly as proud of his battle scars. She found it difficult not to stare and even more difficult to forget the man she lovingly washed. She cursed herself for lingering over the washing process. She cursed herself for remembering old feelings she had for the war-torn hero. Once she rinsed off the soap, Harlan followed through with the drying process, his sad fingers sticking out of casts containing his broken, extensively pinned together bones. He behaved professionally and remained mostly silent while she gave him his bath, although she caught the stray looks he cast at her. She wasn't sure what was going through his mind, but his mind was definitely reeling with information.

Once she had finished washing his upper body, she took a deep breath and hesitated before removing some of the pillows used to prop him in a slightly upright position. Harlan studied her apprehensive look, catching her attention.

"Are we friends?" he asked in an oddly timid tone.

She glanced at him and attempted to keep her cheeks from turning red, which proved useless. "Yes, we're friends."

The way he studied her was almost nerve-racking.

"So this isn't awkward for you?"

Indy couldn't help but smile and managed a nervous laugh. "I assure you, it's very awkward."

"Oh--" he said softly without taking his eyes off her. "Sorry."

Indy reluctantly pulled the covers back, saw what awaited her, and hurriedly pulled the covers back up to his waist. She knew her face was bright red after what she'd just witnessed. If it wasn't enough that she'd now seen Harlan naked, his soldier saluting her was almost enough to send her into panic mode. She had no idea what she was supposed to do.

Harlan offered a tiny, almost embarrassed smile. "I said I was sorry."

Indy shot a look at him, allowing her mouth to fall open with surprise. Despite his attempt at sympathy, she wasn't buying his apology.

"You know, you're like an uncle to me," she finally blurted out as her only recourse to the image burned into her mind.

He suddenly snorted a humored laugh. "Yeah, a dirty perverted uncle."

Indy glared at him. Harlan grinned and chuckled despite her obvious embarrassment. She wondered if it was somehow her fault, because she lingered while washing his battle scars. She suddenly realized she wasn't fully prepared to wash Harlan's private parts, especially in his aroused state. Indy considered her options then met Harlan's gaze. She felt bad, because he wasn't doing it intentionally, but she also needed to put an end to the behavior. She stared into his eyes and removed all sympathy.

"I can just as easily wash you with cold water," she announced boldly.

Harlan stared at her with a look of near shock. "You'd do that? I thought we were friends."

She fidgeted then frowned. “Yes, we’re friends,” she informed him. “That means you need to behave.”

“I’m not purposely misbehaving,” he replied.

Indy knew he meant that. It wasn’t his fault, and she felt bad for suggesting using cold water on him. She drew a deep breath and exhaled slowly.

“I know,” she replied gently. “I’m sorry. Let’s just get this over with.”

Indy pulled the covers back, and, despite what awaited her, she began washing him. Harlan shut his eyes, groaned softly, and squirmed slightly. Indy felt her cheeks become hot and red.

“Stop that,” she huffed.

Chapter Thirteen

The large funeral home and crematorium almost resembled a castle nestled on a hill surrounded by woods and without any homes nearby. The massive yard was well maintained with plants, shrubs, and comforting fountains. The funeral home was located down a back road less than a mile from Indy's house. A newer model hearse was parked beneath the covered, side entrance. It was the following day, and Indy's car was parked outside the main entrance. Within the embalming room, Kale stood over a neatly dressed, older dead man on the metal, prep table. He removed the man's glasses and shoes and set them on the nearby table. Indy sat on an older desk in the corner with her head leaning back against the wall. She was in her own world and barely noticed what Kale was doing.

"What you're going through isn't uncommon, Indy," Kale informed her while keeping his attention focused on the man on the table. "You're having a hard time dealing with your idea of a strong, independent man being reduced to a helpless state. It's understandable."

"I wish it were just that," Indy muttered then ran her fingers through her hair.

She considered if she wanted to discuss the events of the last two mornings with her friend. Kale had a habit of over thinking things, but he would eventually realize there was more bothering her. She reluctantly gave in, deciding to share her problems, and leaned forward on the desktop.

"The visiting nurse quit yesterday morning. Harlan verbally assaulted her," she announced then reluctantly muttered, "maybe even physically. Liz said the agency wouldn't send anyone to replace her without promise that Harlan be sedated."

Kale cast a strange look at her. His confusion was obvious. "What do they honestly think Harlan's capable of doing? I thought the man had two broken arms?"

"Two broken arms, a broken leg, three fractured ribs, head trauma, and more stitches then Frankenstein's monster," she announced with a dreary sigh. "That doesn't change the fact that he knows how to apply minimal pressure for maximum pain."

The look on Kale's face showed his concern toward what she just told him. "Is he dangerous?"

She stared at him with disbelief. "Of course he's dangerous," Indy boldly announced. "It's a job requirement. There are no choirboys enlisted with Delta Force."

"Not what I meant."

"You mean could he unknowingly hurt someone?" she asked while tilting her head. "Yes, there's that risk. He's coming off the drugs, so he's a little cranky. Thank God his casts come off in two weeks."

"I don't understand," Kale remarked and returned to his client. "What will that help?"

"He'll be able to wash himself," she remarked almost too quickly.

Kale suddenly turned and stared at her, his mouth hanging open with a strange realization. "Who's washing him now?"

Indy frowned in response and raised her hand. Kale stared at her with astonishment.

"You're washing him? *All* of him?"

"Someone has to," Indy replied with little reaction and wondered why Kale seemed so stunned. "My father and Jackson draw the line at washing another man's privates."

Kale was silent for a long, uncomfortable moment. "I'm not sure how I feel about you giving sponge baths to your father's military buddy."

"Why should you be uncomfortable?" she suddenly demanded. "You're not the one bathing him."

His glare turned almost demanding. "We're practically dating, Indy," Kale informed her. "Of course it's going to make me uncomfortable. He's only a few years older than me."

Indy stared at him matter-of-fact. His comment had successfully surprised her, and she needed to set the record straight.

"We're *not* practically dating."

She never understood why Kale seemed to think there was something brewing between them. She'd never led him on...ever. Indy reinstated the fact that they were just friends on nearly every occasion. Perhaps it was just wishful thinking on his part.

Kale appeared uncomfortable by her comment and shifted. "Okay, let's not get into this debate right now," he announced then indicated the elderly man on the table. "I have to cremate Mr. Lowell. Why don't I meet you upstairs in the kitchen in a few minutes?"

Indy jumped off the desk as if on command. She wasn't looking forward to another debate on how she and Kale were not a couple. She was growing tired of having to explain that little fact to him. Indy didn't understand how he kept mixing the two. As she headed for the embalming room door, she glanced back at Kale, who undressed the dead, elderly man. Kale avoided looking at her, and she knew it wasn't because he was so engrossed in his work. It was going to be another long afternoon.

†

Indy sat at the kitchen table within Kale's living quarters, huddled over a cup of tea. The funeral home had been in Liz and Kale's family for several generations. Kale and Liz had recently returned home to take over the business after their uncle unexpectedly died from a massive heart attack. Liz took less of an interest in the family business, although she did help out during funerals. Indy never understood why her father moved Liz into their home when she had plenty of living space at the funeral home. Kale now lived in the massive home by himself. Perhaps Kale preferred it that way. Indy liked Liz and didn't mind that she shared her home with her father's girlfriend. However, there were times when Indy felt as if she was the one actually living with Liz. Once her father retired and returned home, it would seem more natural.

Indy heard someone moving around within the house. Kale never locked the door, but she wished he would when he was working in the basement. Anyone could walk in and sneak up on him. Indy knew it was ridiculous to be so suspicious. They lived in a small town and the funeral home was practically in the middle of nowhere. Who would really wander in? And yet there was someone in the house now.

"Hello?" came Margo's voice from down the hall. "Where is everybody?"

She felt relief to the familiar voice of her friend. "Margo, in the kitchen!"

Indy was actually surprised Margo stopped by. She worked during the week, which was where she should be now. Town was the opposite direction. Margo entered the kitchen with a paper bag clutched in her hand. She saw Indy and grinned while holding up the bag.

"Hope you don't mind if I crash your lunch date," Margo teased as she approached.

"It's not a date," Indy scoffed under her breath.

Margo appeared surprised by her friend's surly comment. "Ouch, you're testy today," she announced and raised a curious brow. "Was Harlan *hard* on you this morning?"

Indy glared in response to her friend's humor at her situation. "Not funny," she snarled. "And please don't say anything in front of Kale. He's already seething with jealousy."

"He should be," Margo chirped while setting the bag on the table. "Harlan gets a sponge bath and a hand job, and all Kale gets is a friendly handshake."

"I'm regretting telling you anything," Indy said curtly and glared at her friend. "And I didn't give him a hand job. I barely touched him." She squirmed in her chair. "It's not my fault that guys who abstain for long periods of time are fully loaded with a hairpin trigger."

"So you're saying your house is filled with a bunch of quick draws?" Margo teased.

Indy rolled her eyes at her friend's comment. The image flashing in her mind was enough to make her ill. Margo joined her at the table and removed several sandwiches from the bag.

Despite Margo's grin, she attempted a crude apology. "I'm sorry. I couldn't help myself." She glanced at Indy with a curious look while handing her a sandwich. "You're really bothered by this, aren't you?"

Indy groaned softly and leaned back in her chair. She stared at the sandwich with a lack of appetite.

"Harlan has no idea who I am or even who he is, but he remembered I gave him a sponge bath yesterday," Indy informed her. "He was a little too enthusiastic to see me this morning. It's very uncomfortable having the man I idolized growing up getting excited over me bathing him."

"Harlan doesn't even know his own name," Margo reminded her. "I know you're bothered because he's your father's best friend and someone you've looked up to most of your life, but he's coming off a shitload of painkillers and had his brains scrambled. He's lucky to be alive." She offered a gentle, reassuring smile. "Let him enjoy his sponge baths for another two weeks. He probably won't remember any of it anyway."

"I suppose you're right," Indy replied with a sigh then looked at her friend. "I just wish his wife would offer to help out. It wouldn't be nearly as awkward for her to bathe him."

"Have you heard from her since you brought him home?" Margo asked.

"She called once, but she hasn't stopped by yet," Indy replied then shook her head. "What's her problem? Liz and I were on the next flight out when we heard the guys had been wounded. The least she could have done was show up at the hospital once he was transferred to the states."

Margo shifted in her chair and gently shrugged her shoulders. "Some women make lousy wives."

"You know, when he married her, I thought she was the luckiest woman in the world," Indy announced. "I was so envious of her. Now, I just loathe her. I don't know how she can be so insensitive to the man she married."

Her friend studied her distant expression for a long moment. Margo shifted in her chair then leaned on the table while meeting her gaze.

"Sounds like you're a tad jealous," Margo remarked.

"Of Maureen?" Indy suddenly bellowed and shook her head. "No, absolutely not."

"I meant that she married Harlan," she replied gently. "You had a crush on him when you were a little girl, didn't you?"

Indy frowned and attempted to avoid looking into Margo's eyes. "A little one."

"You love the guy, I get it," Margo replied. "We all have that little girl crush holding a special spot in our hearts."

"Unfortunately, mine has crossed the line the last two mornings," Indy announced. "He's inappropriately aroused by me when he otherwise wouldn't be." She remained uncomfortable. "I'm worried it's stirring up old feelings for him that I'd buried a long time ago."

"And in two weeks," Margo reminded her, "everything will go back to the way it was meant to be. Let him have his fun until his memory resets. He needs you, and you're the reason he's going to recover. Not Maureen."

Chapter Fourteen

After a tense lunch at Kale's house, Indy entered the foyer of her home to find her father sitting at the bottom of the heavily decorated stairs. His hands were clasped between his knees and a frown was chiseled on his face. His expression and posture immediately worried her. She was sensitive to his moods, since he didn't have a wide range to begin with. Had Harlan's unexpected, long-term visit finally destroyed her father's relationship with Liz? Then a more frightening thought occurred to her. Had her father somehow discovered Harlan's off-color behavior during his baths the last two mornings? The thought frightened her. She had no idea how her father would react to that sort of news. Indy gently shut the front door without taking her eyes off him. It frightened her that he hadn't looked up when she entered.

"Is something wrong?" she asked in a tone almost too soft for him to hear.

Flynn groaned softly and flashed a paper he'd been holding. "Maureen filed for divorce," he replied then looked at Indy with something that resembled a sneer on his face. "*Diminished* mental capacity."

Indy felt her heart sink in her chest. “He's still recovering,” she suddenly cried out. The sinking in her heart was immediately replaced with her rising blood pressure. “How can she do that to him?”

Flynn inhaled deeply and straightened where he sat on the step. “Harlan said their relationship had been in doubt for a couple of years,” he announced then finally shook his head with disgust. “I'm going to get a good lawyer to represent his estate. We're going to use our care expenses against Maureen to keep her from cleaning him out.” He ran his hand firmly over his bald head and refrained from cursing, although Indy was sure he wanted to let the profanities fly. “Thank God he's in his own little world right now. I'd hate to break this to him.”

She approached her father on the staircase and attempted to keep her emotions in check. The last thing she needed was to set her father off by spewing her own curse-laced tangent.

“It's going to be fine, Dad,” she informed him in the gentlest tone she could manage. “We'll look after Harlan.”

Flynn smiled at her as he stood and hugged her. She immediately returned the warm embrace. Although his strong arms came close to crushing her, she didn’t complain. Her father could strangle her in his arms like a python, and she wouldn’t complain. She was just happy he was around to hold her. Too often, she feared he’d never return.

“I am so lucky to have such a wonderful daughter,” he announced while clinging to her. “I'll never forget what you're doing for Harlan.” He pulled away and smiled at her. “When he’s back on his feet, I'm going to send you and your friends on a nice vacation.”

“That's not necessary.”

“I know, but I want to do it.” His smile turned into a frown. “You deserve it after having to bathe a grown man.” Flynn chuckled lowly. “Is it wrong that I'm glad it's not me doing it?”

“No, Dad,” she replied and held back her laugh. She couldn’t even imagine her father washing a grown man. “How's he doing this afternoon?”

“He's been in a great mood since this morning,” he replied, thankfully not connecting the dots between Harlan’s bath and his good mood. “Still a little nutty, but I'm thinking about bringing him out to sit with us tonight. It's Christmas Eve. He should be getting up and walking around a little more.”

“I think that’s a wonderful idea,” Indy announced with a pleased smile. “I should probably take him some lunch.”

"Liz took care of that a little while ago. She wanted to help out," he reported then offered a pleased smile. "I think she's finally warming up to the idea of Harlan staying here a while."

"That's a relief," Indy remarked aloud then immediately regretted it.

She didn't want her father to know she had her concerns about Liz's feelings toward Harlan. Flynn gave her a strange look and immediately tilted his head in question.

"Were you worried?"

Indy wanted to avoid responding, but her father would never let it go. When he wanted answers, he used years of interrogation training on her. It was easier just to answer his questions willingly and end her suffering quickly.

"I'd be lying if I said I didn't feel some tension between you and Liz," she replied gently.

"You don't need to worry about me and Liz," he informed her while grinning. "Things between us are just fine."

Indy gave her father a sharp look, because she knew that was a lie. She knew they hadn't been intimate since he returned. Liz wasn't exactly quiet about romantic interludes, which seemed to happen with great frequency. He seemed to understand the look she gave him and both fidgeted with embarrassment. Her father smiled warmly, placed his arm around her shoulder, and indicated the decorations on the staircase.

"You did a beautiful job on the Christmas decorations," he announced, seemingly changing the subject.

Indy frowned at the diversion but allowed him the easy out. "I wanted everything to be perfect," she announced and managed a tiny smile. "You know, the way it used to be."

Flynn nodded and stared at the staircase a moment in silence. "Yes," he replied softly. "It's exactly the way it used to be." He lowered his head and appeared to hold his breath. "And when I walked through the door and saw the decorations 'the way they used to be', I remembered *how* things used to be." He exhaled and trembled slightly. "Until the one Christmas Eve when they changed forever." He was again silent.

Indy stared at him, uncertain what to say. She could feel tears welling up in her eyes as thoughts of her mother dying on this very night flooded her memory. Flynn pulled Indy against his side and held her tightly to him.

"I haven't been able to get your mother out of my head since I returned," he replied softly without looking at her. "I need time to heal, and that's all Liz needs to know."

"I understand," Indy whispered softly and placed her head on her father's shoulder while holding back her own tears.

†

Indy entered Harlan's bedroom just off the family room. She found Harlan comfortably sitting in the easy chair alongside the bed while watching cartoons on the television located within the armoire. His lunch tray set on the table before him untouched. He seemed completely preoccupied with the cartoon. Indy approached him, eyed his lunch tray, and sat on the bed next to his chair.

"Not hungry?"

Harlan didn't respond and stared blankly at the television. Indy looked at the cartoon he'd been intently watching. The dynamite exploded, blowing the fur off the coyote. Harlan twitched in response but didn't take his eyes off the television. Indy took the remote control from his hand and turned the channel. He continued to stare at the detergent commercial without acknowledging her. She wasn't sure if she should be concerned.

"Harlan?"

Harlan finally snapped out of his trance, looked at her, and suddenly grinned boyishly. "Is it bath time?"

His response was moderately disturbing. Out of all the things he could potentially remember, his baths were always the first thing on his mind.

"You have a one-track mind."

He gave her an innocent look as if not even hearing her comment. "The coyote blew himself up."

She tensed slightly by the comment. "I saw," she replied while attempting not to make a big deal out of it. "What are you thinking?"

"He used too much dynamite," he replied without emotion. Harlan again grinned. "Is it bath time?"

"No, Harlan," she informed him firmly while summoning her courage. "Not until morning."

The disappointment clearly showed on his face. "Oh--"

"You weren't hungry?" she asked while indicating the tray.

He didn't bother looking at the tray and showed little reaction. "The coyote poisoned it."

"It's leftover turkey potpie," she quickly announced and couldn't help her feeling of surprise by his odd response. "You love turkey potpie--"

As Indy reached for the tray, Harlan suddenly cast the bowl of potpie away from her hand with force and vigor. The bowl flew across the room and struck the wall. Indy jumped with surprise to his outburst and amazing reflexes. Harlan glared with cold eyes that pierced through her.

"I told you, the coyote *poisoned* it." His comment was so stern and frightening; it startled her.

"Okay--" she timidly replied, feeling fearful from his aggression for a brief moment.

She wasn't sure what had set him off, but she was almost certain it had something to do with the explosion in the cartoon. Indy slowly stood and stared across the room at the mess on the floor and wall. She felt Harlan's fingers touch her bare, lower arm. Indy looked at him with surprise. He stared up at her with a moderately shameful look.

"I'm sorry if I upset you."

Harlan displayed a glimmer of the man she once knew. Indy smiled and affectionately touched his face while staring into his dark eyes. For a moment, she marveled at how handsome he was. She hadn't allowed those feelings to surface since the day he married Maureen.

"We'll get through this, Harlan."

He stared back at her and seemed unusually silent. Something was clearly on his mind, but Indy doubted he even knew what that was.

"Do you love me?" he asked gently.

His words stunned her. Indy slowly kneeled before him and held his fingers exposed beyond his cast.

"Yes, Harlan, I love you," she said softly while staring into his eyes.

She felt a pang of her childhood crush rushing back to her. The way he stared at her send shock waves of lust through her entire body. Indy tensed slightly then forced a smile and swiftly lightened the mood.

"Do you know what tonight is?"

Harlan suddenly grinned. "My bath?"

"No, it's Christmas Eve," she informed him while completely ignoring the bath comment. "The guys and a few friends are coming over tonight. We're going to have a really good time." Thoughts of past Christmas' when her mother was alive flashed through her mind, filling her with untold joy. She smiled more to herself. "Maybe when you see the commander and your comrades drunk something will click."

"Is Nala making eggnog?" he suddenly asked.

Indy felt her entire body tense as she stared at Harlan with surprise. Her heart pounded rapidly in her chest while tears welled in her eyes. She laughed softly and attempted to contain her tears of joy. He'd remembered her mother's name!

"Yes, we'll have my mother's eggnog," she replied while staring at him.

"Nala kissed me under the mistletoe," he announced matter-of-fact. "Don't tell the commander."

Although his comment surprised her, Indy held back her tears of joy and sniffed. "It'll be our little secret."

His boyish grin returned as his eyes lit up. "Will you kiss me under the mistletoe?"

"Yes, Harlan," she announced almost too eagerly. "I most definitely will."

His look turned serious. Something seemed to trouble him. "If I forget, will you remind me?"

Indy smiled, threw her arms around his neck, and hugged him. She was overjoyed by the smallest of memory. Harlan made an effort to cling to her despite his casts. Indy lingered in the feeling of his embrace and wished she didn't ever have to let go.

Harlan gently nuzzled her face with his and sighed softly. "I'm ready for my bath now."

Chapter Fifteen

It was later that afternoon when Indy had joined her father and Liz in the kitchen to help with the feast for the intimate gathering of friends on Christmas Eve. There was enough food cooling on the counter to feed a small country. Flynn mixed a large batch of eggnog while Liz decorated gingerbread men with artistic flair. Indy arranged cheese wedges on a serving tray as she stood opposite her father at the island counter. It was obvious Flynn had been sampling the eggnog while he prepared the liquid joy. A grin crossed his tough face, giving him an almost boyish appearance as he reflected back to an earlier, more joyful time.

"I remember that Christmas," Flynn announced cheerfully. "That had to be eight years ago." He smiled through gritted teeth while looking at Indy. "I remember it distinctly, because I chased Jackson around the house with the broomstick for kissing *you* under the mistletoe."

Indy remembered the incident vividly and had a good laugh about it. It wasn't as if she hadn't kissed the guys under the mistletoe before.

"I'm pretty sure I kissed Nate and Harlan too," she boldly announced in Jackson's defense.

"Maybe so, but I think Jackson kissed you with a little more vigor," Flynn said firmly.

His memory served him correct, allowing Indy to reflect on that particularly Christmas Eve with added fondness. A twisted smile crossed her face as she sank into thought.

"Oh, yeah," Indy announced then chuckled and raised her brows suggestively. "My first French kiss."

Flynn suddenly glared at her. He obviously wasn't humored, and eight years wasn't enough time to heal those wounds. Indy immediately stopped smiling. She didn't want poor Jackson being struck for no apparent reason the next time he walked into the room. Liz had a difficult time keeping a straight face.

"I know it's just a small memory," Indy remarked, "but he remembered something, so that's a good thing."

"Yeah, but why did it have to be kissing your mother?" Flynn sulked and shook his head. "I think I should be a little disturbed by that."

"I wouldn't worry too much about it, Dad," Indy announced while remaining cheerful. "A minute before that he was trying to convince me that a cartoon character poisoned his lunch."

Liz appeared surprised by the comment and suddenly looked at her. "He didn't enjoy the leftover turkey potpie?" she questioned. "But I thought that was his favorite? He had two helpings the other night."

"It's nothing personal, Liz, I promise," Indy replied. "Everyone knows you're an excellent cook."

Liz grinned at the compliment. "Thank you."

As she resumed decorating the cookies, Flynn looked over her shoulder, appeared serious, and pointed at the colorful gingerbread man in her hand. "I think I know that guy."

†

A little later, after dinner, Indy entered Harlan's bedroom while carrying a festive glass of eggnog. Harlan sat on his bedside recliner with the television remote control in his hand. He frantically pressed the on and off button with a vengeance. The television turned on and off with each press of the button, barely keeping up with his rapidly flicking thumb. She gave him an odd look and cast glances from him to the television. The distant look on his face concerned her. She wasn't even sure if he realized she had entered the room.

"It's not working," he announced with some agitation, indicating he was aware of her presence.

She attempted to remain calm and pleasant, so as not to agitate him further. "What are you trying to do?" Indy asked gently while watching him.

"It won't detonate."

Indy set the glass down on the bedside table and watched his repetitive actions with moderate concern. She was somewhat puzzled by the comment.

"Detonate?"

"It should have detonated," he informed her, his brows knitting heavily with anxiety. "Something's wrong. Someone blocked the signal."

Indy's heart sank with understanding. Harlan was reliving some trauma from the explosion that nearly killed him, and it saddened her that she couldn't do anything about it. She gently removed the remote control from his hand, knelt before him, and caressed his legs. He met her sympathetic gaze and seemed to relax slightly to her touch.

"It detonated, Harlan," she announced gently. "You saved them all."

He appeared puzzled. "Saved who?"

Indy attempted a smile and straightened. "Let's change your shirt into something more festive for tonight," she announced, hoping to change the subject to something more cheerful. "Everyone's excited to see you up and about." She handed him the glass of eggnog from the bedside table, which he eagerly accepted. "One glass now and one glass later. I don't want the alcohol interacting with your meds."

Indy turned toward the walk-in closet and removed a Christmas vest and a sporty jacket. She held them up and considered if they matched.

"Oh, damn," Harlan suddenly exclaimed.

Indy quickly turned away from the closet and looked back at him. Harlan had spilled the entire glass of eggnog on his lap. Indy hurried toward him, removed the empty glass from his lap, and looked at his soaked pants.

"Great," she muttered softly.

He looked up at her with a serious gaze. "I think I need a bath."

Indy suddenly shot a look at him as he innocently stared back at her. The look beyond his eyes revealed his more sinister ulterior motive. Her expression suddenly dropped at what she swore was a tiny smirk on his face. She didn't want to admit that he'd spilled his drink on purpose, but something told her it was no accident.

Chapter Sixteen

The gathering was small and informal compared with the extravagant parties the Stryker's were once known to host. Those in attendance consisted of Flynn, Liz, Nate, and Jackson. Indy's friends, Roman and Margo, naturally were present. Liz's brother, Kale, and a couple of her friends were invited as well. Then there was Nate's girlfriend, more fondly known as 'his woman in port', who had arrived for the party. Naturally, Nate's girlfriend was a raving, blonde beauty in her early twenties with large, bouncy breasts. Her festive, red dress was skintight and barely covered her backside, revealing her long, shapely legs only further accented by her daringly high, stiletto heels. Not too surprising, her name was Candy. Nate's girlfriends were almost perfect clones of one another, and it was sometimes hard to distinguish one from the other. Usually, they were of the highest maintenance and flashy wardrobe that screamed 'porn star'. A conversation with one was pretty much like a conversation with another. Although they were never high on intellect, they tended to be bubbly and friendly, making them enjoyable company.

Indy assisted Harlan into the lavishly decorated family room for the holiday gathering. He wore his festive Christmas vest beneath his sporty jacket. Everyone gathered to greet him with Christmas yuletide cheer. Judging by his look, he didn't recognize anyone, even those he'd seen earlier in the day. He came across as polite but slightly suspicious of those within the room, reinforcing the need for an intimate gathering over the entire town showing for the party. Flynn and Nate helped him to an overstuffed chair and propped his casted leg on an ottoman. As his team helped him get settled, Indy approached the bar and filled a glass with eggnog from the large punch bowl. Jackson approached her and immediately noticed her unusual behavior.

"Is something wrong?" Jackson suddenly asked while studying her. "You look flushed."

Indy drank the entire contents of the glass and immediately refilled it. Jackson watched her with his mouth partially open. She wasn't much of a drinker, so her actions were out of the ordinary. Indy glared at Jackson while raising her brows.

"He spilled eggnog on himself and needed to be changed," she remarked lowly, "--and washed."

There was an odd silence as Jackson stared at her with surprise. She immediately regretted telling him when she saw him attempting to hide his grin.

"Well, isn't he the lucky *stiff.*"

She glared at him, immediately wiping the smile from his face. "No pun intended?" she demanded hotly.

Jackson risked her wrath and chuckled. Indy shook her head with disgust.

"I don't care how scrambled his brains are, he did it on purpose," she announced sternly and took another swallow of eggnog. "He was begging for a glass of eggnog all through dinner and before I got him ready for the party. He knew I'd have to wash him or risk him turning sour."

Jackson could barely contain his devious grin. "That's Harlan for you."

"Are you insane?" she suddenly demanded while staring at him. "Harlan *never* acted like that. He's turning into some sort of pervert."

Jackson's look turned serious. "Harlan is extremely intelligent and manipulative."

"I know, but--"

"But nothing," he blurted out defensively. "His moral compass is broken. He's just being a guy and acting on instinct. You are aware that guys are horn balls by nature. You went to college." Jackson casually waved her off. "Sure, he's playing you so you'll play with him, but look at him." He indicated the cheerful man sitting in the overstuffed chair. "He's happy. Five weeks ago, he was practically a dead man. By all accounts, he should be dead." Jackson gave Indy a serious look. "And let's be honest; if I thought I could con you into a hand job, I'd do it too."

"That's disgusting," she scoffed. "You're my friend. Practically my brother."

"Ah, but I'm not your brother, and I'm still a man," he announced then tilted his head with a curious look. "Do you think any less of me?"

She frowned in response. "I'm starting to."

"Personally, I'm thrilled he's plotting ways to get you to manhandle him. It means he's thinking," Jackson remarked. "Pretty soon he's going to remember things. Once he remembers you, everything is going to go back to the way it was." There was an uncomfortable pause as Jackson stared at her. "I just hope you'll spare him the embarrassment of what he's done if he doesn't remember."

She stared at him with a look of annoyance on her face then groaned softly. "God, you're as bad as Margo," she huffed, "but you're absolutely right." Indy suddenly grinned with malicious intent. "And if he spills anything else on his lap tonight, the two of you can clean him up."

Indy patted Jackson's shoulder and walked away.

†

Although not the grand Christmas parties of the good old days, the small gathering was starting to resemble something of a Stryker Christmas party past. Nate was almost always the first one to get drunk and out of hand. Sadly, her father was usually not far behind, although, he managed to maintain a certain degree of discretion that Nate lacked. Indy was usually mindful of Jackson when he started drinking. He would turn up the charm and become excessively affectionate toward her, which usually ended with her father and Jackson getting into a pissing match. In an unusual change of events, Margo struck up a conversation with Jackson, and his attention seemed to focus on her instead. Indy, feeling oddly as if she were interrupting some secret bout of foreplay, slipped away from Margo and Jackson. She joined Roman, who was engaged in a rather heated debate with Nate. She wasn't sure what the debate involved, but she feared that if Nate became too animated, he might pulverize poor Roman. It wasn't that she felt any degree of sympathy toward Roman, because he knew the consequences of engaging in any form of controversial debate with a drunken Nate was considered a bad idea. Nate's girlfriend, Candy, stood idly by and witnessed the ensuing conversation with little emotion. Indy paused alongside Candy and listened to the two men talking loudly in animated discussion.

"No, no," Roman boldly announced in a tone louder than necessary.

Indy held her breath. It was never wise for a man to raise his voice around Nate in debate. It would only turn the conversation into a louder pissing match.

"You have to pretreat the stain before you put it in the washing machine," Roman remarked. "Once you put it in the dryer, you've essentially baked the stain into your shirt."

"I did pretreat the stain," Nate loudly announced. "All I got was big white spots all over my clothes."

Roman groaned, covered his eyes, and shook his head. "Nate, you don't pretreat with bleach. That only applies to whites. Of course your clothes turned white."

Indy stared at the men with her mouth slightly open. Were they debating washing clothes? What messed up world had she just entered? She looked at Candy, who appeared mostly bored.

"Are they serious?"

"Please, make it stop," Candy muttered to Indy. "They've been talking laundry the last twenty minutes. If I wanted to talk about clothing, I would have gone to my brother's 'ugly sweater' party. At least that's funny. This is just sad."

"You're not kidding," Indy remarked. "This is usually the part where I step in and break up the fight. I've got this though."

"Thank you," Candy gasped softly while batting excessively long lashes.

Indy linked onto Roman's arm and leaned into him, distracting him from the conversation. He looked at her and appeared curious by her actions.

"I need your opinion on something," Indy announced in a soft tone.

Roman was immediately curious and excused himself. Indy led him a few feet across the room, released his arm, and then casually indicated Margo and Jackson flirting like schoolchildren at a high school dance.

"Is Margo actually flirting with Jackson?" Indy asked.

Roman stared at the couple a moment and watched as Margo placed her hand on Jackson's lower arm while laughing at something he'd said.

"It certainly looks that way," Roman replied, although he appeared unconvinced. "But that can't be, because that's Margo. She doesn't flirt. She's been boasting celibacy since I'd met her."

"I know," Indy announced. "Ever since that bad breakup right before she started college. Honestly, Roman, I thought Margo was just using her bad breakup as an excuse to hide the fact that she was a lesbian."

Roman snorted a laugh while grinning. "Yeah, I've fantasized about that too."

Indy glared at Roman and slapped his arm. He yelped softly and rubbed his arm. Both looked back at the happily flirting couple. Indy was momentarily preoccupied.

"She knows he's a bit of a lady's man," Indy remarked. "I mean, I did mention that about a dozen times."

"As her friends," Roman announced, "we should probably keep an eye on her. If she's been drinking, we certainly can't allow her to do something she'll later regret."

"That's what's weird," Indy informed him. "She's not drunk. She's been nursing that same glass of eggnog from the time she arrived."

"You're right," Roman replied. "That is weird."

Kale soon joined them. He had a strange look on his face and gave a general nod toward Jackson and Margo.

"Is Margo flirting with Jackson?" Kale asked. "Did she suddenly switch teams?"

†

Indy entered the kitchen through the family room archway with an empty tray that once contained tasty h'orderves. Liz was leaning on the island counter, sobbing softly. Indy stared a moment with some surprise and then debated whether or not she should intrude on Liz's privacy. She understood that sometimes women just needed to cry. Indy made her decision and approached the island counter, startling Liz. She quickly dried her eyes and attempted to cover that she'd been crying, although her slightly mussed mascara gave her away.

"Is everything okay?" Indy gently asked as she paused only a couple of feet away.

Liz sniffed and covered with a smile. "Yeah, I'm just a little emotional, that's all. It's been a tough few weeks."

"I understand," Indy replied in a soft tone. She understood more than Liz realized. She again debated if she should leave her father's girlfriend to her solitude, but it just wasn't in Indy's nature to allow someone to suffer alone. "You know," Indy began, "my father tends to keep things bottled inside. Sometimes, with big things, he just needs to work through them."

Liz returned her attention to Indy and stared at her a long moment. "He keeps saying he needs time to recover," she replied gently. "I understand, but I keep feeling he's pushing me from his life."

"That's not the case," Indy informed her gently. "He's feeling a lot of emotions, and that's not who he is. It's foreign to him. He loves you, I know he does."

Liz managed a tiny laugh and forced a smile. "I wish he'd show it," she remarked then turned serious. "He hasn't *touched* me since he's been back. I've tried giving him space, but he always seems to be somewhere else."

"He'll come around," Indy promised then smiled knowingly. "He's had nearly a gallon of eggnog, so he's good and mellow right about now. I think you'll find him surprisingly affectionate this evening, if you just give him a chance."

Liz smiled and nodded as she wiped her eyes. "I'll take your advice."

"You may want to freshen up a little," Indy announced and timidly indicated the running mascara beneath her eyes. "You, uh, have a little runoff."

Liz dabbed beneath her eyes then chuckled softly. "Yeah, I think I'll do that."

Chapter Seventeen

Later that evening, Jackson helped Harlan back into the lounge from a trip to the hallway half-bath. Harlan was unusually unsteady on his feet, more so than he had been, and appeared almost drunk. Indy saw the way Harlan was walking alongside Jackson and approached them with concern on her face. Harlan was delighted to see her and reacted animatedly.

"Oh, the pretty lady," Harlan suddenly exclaimed in a cheerful tone that conveyed his obviously drunken condition. "Is it bath time?"

Indy felt her cheeks immediately redden from the blurted comment. She hoped her father hadn't overheard his enthusiastic outburst.

"We've got a live one here," Jackson muttered.

"What happened?" Indy suddenly demanded while glaring at Jackson. "Is he drunk?"

"Don't look at me," Jackson protested with an innocent look on his face. "I only gave him one glass."

"Margo said she gave him his one glass earlier," Indy announced sternly.

"The bald guy gave me a glass," Harlan announced then considered. "The pretty boy gave me a glass." He chuckled softly while attempting to recall the events of the evening. "The big guy gave me a glass." He then considered and grinned. "And his pretty girlfriend gave me a glass."

"God, he's drunk," Indy muttered with disgust.

Harlan chuckled at the expression on her face then looked up to the family room archway where the mistletoe proudly hung above them. He gasped with enthusiasm, pointed to the mistletoe, and grinned slyly.

"You're supposed to kiss under the mistletoe, Nala," Harlan announced then placed his finger to his lips in secrecy. "Don't tell the commander."

Jackson appeared surprised and looked from Harlan to Indy. "Did he just call you by your mother's name?"

There were more pressing matters than his recall of her mother at the moment. Indy needed to figure out a way to get him sober, so he wouldn't fall on his face later.

"I'm going to get him some water," Indy remarked with disgust. "See if you can get him back to his chair."

Indy hurried away from them and approached the bar between the family room and the kitchen. Harlan frowned, pointed to the mistletoe above him, and then to Indy while seemingly pouting at her departure.

"She promised," he remarked.

"Yeah, she's a tease," Jackson muttered.

Harlan suddenly grinned and raised his brows lustfully. "She loves me."

"Do you even know her name?" Jackson firmly asked while cocking his head to the side.

Harlan considered the question with considerable seriousness then grinned deviously. "Want to blow up something?"

Jackson appeared set back by the comment. "Well, at least you're sounding more like the Harlan I remember." He then assisted Harlan back to his chair. Once he had him settled, he pointed a warning finger at him. "Now, behave yourself. I'm going to get you something to eat."

Jackson left Harlan to relax in his chair as he hurried to the kitchen for the buffet. Indy walked around the bar with a bottle of water in her hand. She was still fuming about Harlan's current, drunken state when her father greeted her by the bar with his own slightly drunken grin.

"Kale was just telling me about his work at the mortuary," Flynn announced.

Indy made a face of detest at the comment. "Not in detail, I hope."

"Every gory detail," Flynn replied while grinning.

She held back her groan. Kale enjoyed grossing out people with his funeral home tales almost as much as her father enjoyed telling his stories about how he came to lose two toes.

"Could you do me a favor and spread the word that Harlan is officially off the eggnog for the rest of the night?" Indy asked, hoping her father was sober enough to complete the assignment. "If he throws up, I'm not cleaning it."

Flynn appeared surprised by the comment. "I thought he was only allowed one glass."

"Yeah, and apparently *everyone* gave him one glass."

Her father snorted in response, apparently finding the situation humorous. There was no chance he was going to play the adult tonight.

"Ah, lighten up," Flynn announced and placed his arm affectionately around her shoulder. "He needs to unwind more than any of us. I'll be responsible for him tonight. You just let me handle him."

A glass was heard shattering in sync with a female scream that silenced the room. Indy and her father spun toward the commotion. Harlan, now on his feet, stood before Liz with her wrist clutched in his fingers. A shattered glass of eggnog lie on the floor several feet from them. Flynn, Indy, and Jackson ran to them. Without hesitation, Flynn easily unlocked Harlan's grip on Liz's wrist. He pulled Liz away from Harlan and into his arms. The look on Flynn's face was stunned and almost unpredictable. Harlan suddenly lunged for them, surprising everyone. Jackson stepped into Harlan's path and attempted to stop his charge. Harlan karate punched Jackson in the abdomen with amazing reflexes then swept his legs out from beneath him, despite almost knocking himself to his knees as a result. Jackson roughly struck the floor, unsuccessfully stopping Harlan, as he lunged for the couple.

Indy suddenly jumped in front of Harlan as he swung at Liz and Flynn. She then realized the position she'd put herself into and attempted to deflect his flying fist, but she was a little too slow. Harlan stopped just short of hitting Indy, obviously not his intended target. He appeared slightly alarmed and quickly pulled his fist back. His eyes were wide with concern as he darted glances around the room like a madman.

"Did you see the coyote?" Harlan demanded.

Indy released her breath and held her chest as her heart pounded from the near miss. Had he actually connected with her face, she would have been on the floor alongside Jackson. It took a minute for her to collect herself and regain her composure.

"No, I must have missed it," she gasped softly, still seeing her life flash before her eyes.

Jackson slowly moved to his feet and rubbed his abdomen while eyeing Harlan. "That felt like old times," he muttered, clinging to the arm of the chair.

Indy gently linked onto Harlan's casted arm and attempted to guide him away from the party as quickly as possible. There was only one thing she could think to say that would get him to move faster.

"How about we visit the mistletoe on the way back to your room?"

Harlan's mood immediately lightened as he grinned his approval while patting her lower arm with his fingers. "I'd like that." Despite his unsteadiness, he practically dragged her to the archway with the mistletoe.

"Maybe we could watch a Christmas movie before bed like we used to do," Indy suggested.

Harlan suddenly grinned and looked at her with childlike fascination. "*The Grinch Who Stole Christmas*?"

Surprisingly, that was the one they usually watched. His small memory wasn't enough to overshadow her concerns and the way her father was staring at his best friend and comrade as they crossed the room.

"Yeah, that's the one."

Although attempting to avoid it, Indy met her father's gaze. Flynn held Liz in his arms and gave Harlan a strange look as they passed. She appeared concerned by his unpredictable look as they approached the archway leading into the safety of the back hallway. Harlan stopped her in the archway, smiled, and indicated the mistletoe. It was possibly the only thing he wasn't about to forget. Indy knew everyone was staring, but she had promised him, and above all else, she needed to keep him as calm as possible. She kissed him quickly but warmly on the lips. She hated to admit she enjoyed it, despite everything that had just happened. As she pulled away, her mind momentarily reeling, Harlan slipped his arm around her waist, pulled her against him, and kissed her more passionately. His passionate kiss was enough to send a wave of lust throughout her entire body. She had to resist returning the kiss out of fear she might be unwilling to control her own desire.

Everyone was now staring at them with their mouths hanging open. Flynn released Liz and made a motion toward them. Jackson grabbed his arm, risking bodily harm, and stopped him. Harlan broke off the kiss and smiled boyishly at Indy. She stared back at him a moment with surprise to the passionate and aggressive kiss. It was enough to shock her, momentarily causing her to freeze. She could almost feel her father's stare cutting through them. Indy uncertainly smiled while attempting to slow her rapid heart rate, took Harlan's arm, and quickly guided him to the hallway in the direction of the spare bedroom. She needed to put as much distance between Harlan and her father as possible.

Chapter Eighteen

Nearly an hour after Harlan's 'freak-out' at the party, Indy returned to the kitchen and filled a plate with snacks for her and Harlan. Despite the minor gap in time, Harlan didn't seem to remember any of what had happened. Indy was feeling the weight of the last few days beating her down, and she didn't know how much more she could take. With his most recent outburst, she was certain her plight to keep Harlan in the house would soon be outnumbered by those who considered him a threat. She could hear the small gathering of their few friends having a good time in spite of Harlan's floorshow. The family room was just beyond the large archway into the kitchen only separated by the massive wet bar, but, to her surprise, she could hear her father and Liz outside the kitchen doorway leading into the hallway. She wasn't sure why they were in the hallway rather than the family room with the others, but she suspected it was to conduct a private conversation. It wasn't in her nature, but Indy felt compelled to listen to their conversation beyond the door. She was almost positive their little talk had something to do with Harlan.

"It's only been a few days," Flynn assured Liz in a firm yet comforting tone. "He needs time, that's all."

"He needs to be committed," Liz snapped hotly. "Maybe he's not crazy in the traditional sense, but he's going to hurt someone. He nearly broke my wrist, almost hit Indy, and took down Jackson. Do you need a bigger red flag?"

There was an awkward silence. Indy knew exactly what words were about to come out of her father's mouth, since she'd heard them time and again.

"The man saved my life."

"I'm aware of that, but you can't let him kill you because you owe him one," Liz informed him.

"More like three," Flynn muttered.

"You know what I mean," Liz countered then became unusually quiet, concerning Indy as she eavesdropped. "I didn't want to say anything, but I'd heard some disturbing things about his behavior during his baths."

Indy felt her heart suddenly stop then pound in response. How could Liz possibly know? She hadn't told Kale. Only Jackson and Margo were given that information. She couldn't imagine either of them telling Liz. Although, if Jackson opened his big mouth to Kale, that would explain everything. Indy cursed both Kale and Jackson softly under her breath.

"What sort of disturbing things?" Flynn suddenly asked in a tone that nearly sent Indy's neck hairs on end.

"Apparently he's been masturbating while she washes him," Liz informed him.

The words outraged Indy. She knew that wasn't true, but the allegation would be enough to cost Harlan his happy home. There was an awkward silence. Indy waited for the explosion. She could only imagine the look on her father's face. To her surprise, the explosion never came.

"He needs to be in a hospital," Liz announced firmly.

And then came the words that terrified Indy most.

"It's him or me, Flynn."

Indy felt her heart sink. Harlan's fate was practically sealed the moment the words left Liz's mouth. She wanted to hate Liz, but she could understand her concerns, since she wasn't as close to Flynn's men as Indy was. Indy held back her tears while feeling her entire body become weak.

"Can we talk about this later?" Flynn asked softly.

A moment passed, telling Indy they were on their way into the kitchen. She quickly returned to filling her plate with snacks for the

Christmas Eve movie hour as the kitchen door opened. Indy placed two napkins on the tray despite her trembling hands and forced a smile while she greeted her father as he approached. She assumed Liz returned to the party, avoiding the kitchen. Flynn paused by the island counter, gave Indy a strange look, and appeared concerned by her expression. She had tried to cover as best she could, but it was hard keeping things from her father.

"Are you okay?" Flynn asked while studying her.

"I'm fine," she chirped a little too quickly and in a pitch higher than normal.

His look was almost sympathetic, as if he was about to put down her beloved pet. "Did you want me to stay with Harlan this evening?"

"No, we're good," she replied abruptly, then cursed herself for having said it in that tone.

"There's something I need to ask you, Indy," he announced, causing alarm to sweep through her body. As he stared into her eyes, every muscle in her body tensed. Her father was clearly uncomfortable. "Has Harlan been behaving inappropriately toward you during his baths?"

She held her breath to refrain from answering too quickly and arousing suspicion. She added a reassuring smile in an attempt to put him at ease.

"Nothing I can't handle."

Flynn didn't appear convinced and wasn't about to let it go. "Has he done something?" he demanded.

Indy casually shrugged while maintaining her tiny smile. "He might enjoy his baths a little too much, but it's nothing personal. I can handle it."

His look was stern. "Are you sure?"

"Yes, I'm sure."

Indy waited for the explosion she still felt certain would follow, but it never came. Her father seemed very uncomfortable, and he didn't have to tell her why. She knew. He finally drew a deep breath and straightened proudly but lacked conviction.

"We need to have a serious discussing about Harlan tomorrow," he informed her.

Indy could feel her entire body start to tremble in time with her pounding heart. She could almost feel the tears welling up inside her eyes. Despite her emotions, she managed to convey a calm outward demeanor.

"I'd better get back to the movie."

Indy held back her tears, picked up her tray, and hurried from the kitchen toward the connecting hallway door. It wasn't the quickest way to the guest bedroom, but she could avoid the small crowd in the family room. She didn't need her father's men seeing her cry.

Chapter Nineteen

Indy sat in the recliner alongside the king-sized bed while Harlan remained comfortably propped in a sitting position on top of the comforter. She had changed him into a comfortable pair of shorts and a t-shirt, which he could also sleep in if it got too late. Both watched the movie and picked at the food on the tray setting on the rolling table between them. Harlan cheerfully sang along with the song, "You're A Mean One Mr. Grinch". Indy felt compelled to stare at him and almost couldn't take her eyes off him. She felt sadness overcome her. She fought her tears and looked away from both him and the television. Despite the continuing song, Harlan no longer sang. Indy looked back at him. He stared at her with a serious look as if he had read her mood. She attempted to wipe her tears away unnoticed.

"It's okay," Harlan announced sympathetically, "he returns the presents."

Indy attempted to smile at his childlike innocence. He had no idea what was about to happen. Perhaps he wouldn't even be affected by the move. That small part of him struggling to break free seemed to be buried deep inside. Harlan moved over on the bed and patted the empty spot alongside him. Indy joined him on the bed without hesitation, clung to his arm as if she'd never let go, and rested her head on his shoulder. Harlan appeared pleased and caressed her arm clinging to his. Indy fought her tears and tried to maintain her composure, but it was difficult. She kept thinking about what happened to Harlan and how she thought they'd lose him. She couldn't stop from speaking her thoughts.

"It nearly killed me when I thought you might die," she said softly, wanting so badly to share her feelings with him.

He gave her a puzzled look. "When was that?"

Indy drew a deep breath, knowing he didn't understand what she was talking about, and refrained from looking at him.

"When you went boom."

Although she couldn't look at him, she knew he was staring at her. She caught a glimpse of the look in his eyes and immediately placed her attention back on the movie. He continued to stare at her with all seriousness.

"I'm sorry I upset you like that," he announced then gently wiped the tears from her face.

Indy tensed to his fingers gently touching her face. She hated to admit his touch sent shock waves through her. She hated to admit that she'd been in love with Harlan, and that those feelings never went away no matter how much she lied to herself that they had. Indy knew she couldn't look at him. She couldn't gaze into his dark eyes. She knew what she'd see, and she couldn't allow those emotions to surface. She nuzzled his shoulder and clung to his arm. His exposed fingers outside his cast gently caressed her lower arm, making her want to crawl inside him. She'd always felt so safe when she was with him. She never wanted to know a life without Harlan in it.

"I can't bear the thought of losing you, Harlan," she whispered softly and immediately regretting saying it aloud.

"Am I going somewhere?" he immediately inquired.

He may have suffered traumatic memory loss and had his brains slightly scrambled, but there was no escaping Harlan's astounding perception. It seemed to be one of the few traits he retained despite his injuries.

Indy sniffed, nuzzled his shoulder, and attempted a tiny smile. "Not if I have a say."

Harlan gently pulled away from her arms clinging to his and placed his arm securely around her shoulder. Without hesitation, Indy moved against his chest and clung to him, contented just to listen to his heart beating. He'd held her many times throughout her life. He held her as a child, as a teenager, and as an adult. There was no place she'd rather be. She just wanted him to hold her in his arms forever.

†

As the closing movie credits rolled, Indy woke to the dim glow of the television. She was suddenly aware that the pillows had been removed from the head of the bed, and she was now lying on her back on the mattress. Harlan lie partially on top of her while warmly kissing her neck and caressing her hip and thigh with his fingers. Indy gasped with surprise by her current position and instinctively pushed against Harlan's shoulders in an attempt to hold him back. She didn't know why he was kissing her or what had possessed him, but this wasn't the man she knew. Despite her resistance, Harlan brushed his lips past hers and then kissed her warmly but passionately. She couldn't deny it felt wonderful while immediately cursing her body for aching against his. She could feel his arousal pressing against her hip in a gentle and loving manner. Indy attempted to break off the kiss, although her arms weren't pushing nearly as hard as she felt they should. She didn't like that she was prolonging his advances, giving her body added time to react with appropriate pleasure. She wasn't even sure if it was evident she was protesting. Her hands against his shoulders seemed to be firmly caressing rather than actually pushing.

"Harlan--" she softly managed to protest.

Harlan's hand ran firmly along her bare leg while sliding her dress upward as he caressed her thigh. Despite the tingling sensation created by his touch, the edge of his cast gently scraped her leg, reminding her he wasn't in his right mind. He positioned himself on top of her and gently moved his hips against hers. With only his shorts and her thin dress between them, she could easily feel every curvature of his arousal pressing in her most sexually arousing spots. Harlan easily maneuvered his lower body between her legs and continued pressing his hips against hers with a certain gentleness yet maintaining purpose. Indy gasped slightly as the hardness of his body easily pressed through her dress and panties. She finally pushed against his shoulders and attempted to hold him back despite his determined gentle thrusts against her. Indy managed to break off the kiss, which she questioned if she had actually been returning it. Harlan immediately sought her neck and kissed her it in all the right places while allowing his arousal to press into her with more determination and desire.

Indy squirmed beneath him. The sensation was too much. All she could think about was how much she wanted to feel him invading her; how she wanted him to take her as she had fantasized so many times before. She clung to him and softly moaned her pleasure, encouraging him further. Harlan slipped his hands along her hips beneath her panties and attempted to slide them off. Indy suddenly returned to reality, realized what she was doing, and caught his hand to stop him.

"No, we can't," she gasped softly, nearly out of breath from her rising lust and the aching in her body.

"Give one good reason," he whispered softly into her ear in a moderately playful tone.

"We're not in that type of relationship," she whispered without conviction.

"We love each other," he announced gently and finally looked into her eyes through the dim glow of the television. "When you touch me, it reminds me I'm alive."

Indy stared into his dark eyes just inches from hers. He *was* alive. He had survived, and right now, that was all that mattered to her. She released his hand partially beneath her panties, shut her eyes, and clung to him. He was right. She loved him, and he was about to be taken from her. Tonight, she wouldn't deny him what he wanted most...perhaps what she wanted most.

Chapter Twenty

It was early Christmas morning. An exhausted Indy was slumped over the kitchen island counter with a cup of tea in front of her and her head in her hands. She heard slow but steady footfalls descending the back, kitchen stairs. She didn't have to look to the stairs behind her, she knew by the sound of the footfalls it was her father. He walked heavy and slow in the morning, especially after a night of too much holiday cheer. Indy immediately tensed. They were going to have the one conversation she didn't want to have regarding Harlan. Unfortunately, the events of last night in Harlan's room still had her mind reeling with every imaginable emotion and overshadowed all else. She somehow feared her father would know what happened between her and Harlan. She felt even more guilt-ridden than she had after losing her virginity in college. The thought of confronting her father this morning was frightening on so many levels. Flynn shuffled into the kitchen with little enthusiasm and kissed her on the head.

"Merry Christmas, dear," he announced in an attempt to sound cheerful despite his hung-over state, which was combined with what was undoubtedly a foul mood regarding Harlan's behavior toward Liz at the party.

"Merry Christmas, Dad," she replied with little enthusiasm.

He shuffled past her, approached the coffeepot, and poured a cup of coffee. Despite not being a coffee drinker, Indy had made a fresh pot as part of her morning ritual. Her father's men were always more pleasant to be around in the morning after they've been successfully caffeinated. It was wise to keep a fresh pot readily available in the morning whenever her father and his men were around. She already knew it was going to be a bad morning, so she wanted to put him in as good a mood as possible. Flynn glanced at her several times while pouring his coffee. She could almost feel his gaze upon her. She could sense that he somehow knew she'd slept with Harlan! It wouldn't help her case to keep him from being committed, that much was evident.

"Why do you look like I feel?" he finally asked.

"I had trouble sleeping," she replied softly and avoided looking at him.

It hadn't been a total lie. She finally lifted her head and stared at her father where he stood by the main counter. He sipped his coffee and appeared to be lost in another world. She decided to go for a direct assault and plead her case for Harlan's freedom. Indy gathered her courage, straightened proudly, and locked eyes with her father.

"Dad, about Harlan's behavior last night--"

Flynn frowned and groaned softly. "Yeah, he's going to need to see the doctor about possible sedation," he announced as he casually sank against the main counter. "After all we've been through; I'd hate to have to hit him."

Indy stared at her father with surprise by the calmness of his remark and his jovial nature. "You mean you're not committing him?" she nearly gasped.

"Committing him?" he suddenly demanded and looked at her with surprise clearly on his face. "No, of course not!" He then hesitated while staring at her. "You still want to take care of him, don't you?"

She was stunned by the direction their conversation had gone and had to fumble with her answer. "Well, yes, of course, but I thought Liz--"

Her father suddenly tensed and again avoided looking at her. Something was clearly on his mind.

"About Liz--" he announced in an oddly timid tone. "Once the guys roll out of bed, we're moving her back home with Kale."

Indy almost felt her heart stop beating in her chest. She couldn't believe what she was hearing. Somehow, Harlan won! The realization of what he said finally hit her, and the threat to his own happiness was devastating.

"She's moving out on Christmas day?"

"It was her decision," he replied in a casual, matter-of-fact tone that surprised her.

Indy held her breath while feeling awful for her father. "Is it because of Harlan?"

He drew a deep breath and met her gaze. "I'm afraid so, honey." Flynn straightened proudly as if about to bellow out orders to the men. His look was stern and unfaltering. "I'm not sending him to some hospital; not as long as we can take care of him." His brave front ended as quickly as it had started. "I've known Liz for ten months. Harlan's been family for fifteen years."

"I'm sorry about Liz, Dad," she said gently, "but thank you for Harlan."

"As long as you can handle his mood swings and sudden hormonal rushes--" her father announced then fell silent and stared at her almost demandingly as if awaiting her response to his silent question.

"We'll be fine," she announced and offered a tiny, pleased smile. "Less than two weeks until his casts come off; then he can start showering himself."

Flynn chuckled softly, appearing moderately amused for some odd reason. It was short-lived. "Until then, feel free to give his boys a swift smack if he gets out-of-line."

Indy felt the need to laugh but held it back. "I'll keep that in mind."

†

After her conversation with her father in the kitchen, Indy knew she now had to face the reality of what happened last night with Harlan. She stopped outside the partially open guest bedroom doorway, took a deep breath, and gathered her courage. She lightly tapped on the door while pushing it open. Indy uncertainly entered the bedroom and glanced toward the bed, where Harlan silently waited. He sat up in bed, shirtless, while reclined against the headboard with two spare pillows behind his back, and the sheets pulled up to his waist. It was obvious, at least to her, that he was naked beneath the covers. Indy forced herself to wipe any dirty thoughts from her mind, but it was difficult. She remembered every detail of their lovemaking. Despite the rough edges of his casts leaving small abrasions on many areas along her skin, he was surprisingly gentle yet amazingly passionate. Her head was left spinning from his sexual competence, and how he'd made her feel. It was the single most erotic moment of her life...and she knew it could never happen again.

Even with Maureen filing for divorce, it was still wrong. He wasn't in his right mind. Most importantly, he was her father's best friend and team member for the last fifteen years out of his seventeen-year tour. As she stared at his broad shoulders and moderately scarred chest, she felt her body ache for him. She needed to stop those feelings! Harlan hadn't even realized she had entered the room. He held the television remote control and pressed the on and off button with frustration. The television turned on and off in response to his frantic, repetitive actions. Indy approached him in the bed. Her desire from last night suddenly waned as she watched him pushing the button to no avail, the frustration clearly on his confused face. The man she loved was off in another world, attempting to save it, while completely unaware that he already had.

"Won't detonate?" she asked sympathetically.

He didn't look at her, but instead stared at the remote as he pressed the button repeatedly and with added vigor. His shattered look saddened her.

"I don't know what happened," he replied while repeatedly reliving his nightmare.

Indy gently took the remote control from him and turned on cartoons. She felt bad that she was treating him almost like a child, but the cartoons relaxed him. Perhaps the soothing effect was from some fond childhood memory. His attention shifted, finally allowing him to look at her, and he grinned in response.

"Is it bath time?"

"Yes, it's bath time."

Indy felt concern, having to explain to him her inappropriate response to last night's advances. She knew he would be in full lust mode after their exploits, and she'd have to find a way to tell him what happened couldn't be repeated. She also needed to curb his desire while she bathed him, because she didn't need the added reminder of what they'd done. It was going to be difficult enough for her after what happened. He stared at her with boyish innocence and indicated the sheets covering him.

"I seem to have misplaced my clothes."

Something suddenly struck Indy. Was it possible he didn't remember last night? He remembered his baths, so surely he'd remember their passionate night together. Indy slowly sat on the edge of the bed and offered a curious smile. She had to know for sure, but she needed to approach it with caution. Memory loss or not, Harlan was still the smartest man she'd ever known. She couldn't risk giving something away that he didn't need to worry about at the moment.

"Do you remember what today is?"

Harlan sank deep into thought and carefully considered the question. He struggled for a response then finally looked at her and grinned as his eyes lit up.

"Bath day?"

Indy gently cleared her throat, held back her laugh, and offered a tiny smile. He didn't remember! She could feel her entire body sag with relief.

"It's Christmas," she replied.

Harlan suddenly grinned in response. "I kissed Nala under the mistletoe last night," he boldly announced. "Don't tell the commander."

"I won't," she replied warmly then smiled. "Merry Christmas, Harlan."

Indy leaned forward and kissed Harlan affectionately on the cheek. She pulled back and met his gaze, staring almost helplessly into his eyes. He stared back at her with a familiar fondness then gently touched her arm with his fingers and returned the smile.

"Merry Christmas, Indy."

Indy's heart suddenly pounded to her name escaping his lips. She stared at him with surprise. It was a mixture of enthusiasm and fear that he possibly remembered what they'd done.

"You remembered my name," she gasped then smiled while fighting her tears of joy. His recovery was more important than whether or not he remembered making love to her. "That's probably the best Christmas present I've ever gotten."

Harlan suddenly grinned and indicated his cast. "I wrote it down last night."

Indy took his fingers in her hand and looked at the writing he'd scribbled on his cast. Although, she didn't remember him doing that, it read, 'Indy--pretty bath girl'. She appeared humored and held his fingers while staring into his eyes. It was now time to be direct with him about what he actually remembered from last night. She needed to be certain what he did and didn't remember.

"Do you remember the party last night?"

"Was it someone's birthday?"

"Jesus' birthday," she offered then tilted her head. "Do you remember what movie we watched after the party?"

"*The Grinch*?"

Indy's heart raced as she stared at him. She attempted to keep from reacting. "Oh, you remember watching that?"

Harlan casually indicated the DVD box on the nightstand. "Lucky guess."

Indy saw the movie box and hid her smile. She was once again relieved. Thankfully, no one would ever have to know what happened. It would be her secret...forever, if necessary.

Chapter Twenty-one

Later Christmas morning, Jackson was slumped over his coffee at the kitchen island counter. He looked like hell after a night of overindulgence of more than just eggnog. Indy entered the kitchen through the archway with a freshly washed and dressed Harlan clinging to her arm. Indy immediately noticed Jackson and his mood. It was a familiar sight from many a Christmas past. For her father's men, Christmas morning was a day of recovery. At least some things never changed. Harlan was surprisingly alert and cheerful, despite his excessive Christmas cheer from last night. Thankfully, he hadn't gotten sick on the potent, milky drink. Indy helped Harlan onto the kitchen chair alongside Jackson. Jackson eyed Harlan, noted his cheerful disposition, and chuckled. It was possible Jackson was jealous that his friend felt better than he did that morning.

"You're in a good mood, Harlan," Jackson announced then grinned slyly and raised his brows in suggestion. "Did you enjoy your bath?"

"Yes, thank you," Harlan replied a little too quickly.

Indy smacked Jackson's shoulder as she passed behind him on her way to the main counter. She prepared a cup of tea for both her and Harlan.

"Wish my Christmas morning started off on that note," Jackson playfully pouted while barely containing his lustful grin. "What did you kids do last night?"

Indy tensed with her back to Jackson and tried to brush the sexual images from her mind.

"We watched a movie," she casually replied.

"We slept together," Harlan informed him.

Jackson nearly choked on his coffee and whipped his head in Harlan's direction. Indy turned toward the island counter with a shocked look. Had she heard him correctly? Jackson looked from Harlan to Indy and then back to Harlan.

"You *slept* together?"

Harlan casually indicated some writing on his cast. "Yes, I wrote it here."

Jackson looked at Harlan's cast where he indicated. It read, 'slept with Indy'. There was a series of numbers written on the cast as well. Jackson gave Indy a stunned look and appeared unable to blink.

"You *slept* with Harlan?"

Indy felt her body tense as her heart raced, but she managed to keep a straight face. "Slept...as in I fell asleep in his bed."

Harlan looked at his cast and appeared bewildered. It was obvious he was giving the entire conversation a little too much consideration.

Jackson exhaled, held back his grin, and laughed softly. "You had me concerned a minute there."

Indy placed Harlan's tea on the counter before him. Jackson eyed the numbers written on Harlan's cast.

"What's with the numbers?"

"I'm not sure," Harlan replied while studying them, struggling to remember.

"They're detonation codes," Indy replied casually and leaned on the counter across from them.

Harlan and Jackson looked at Indy with shared surprise to her assessment. She stared back at them then laughed at their priceless expressions.

"He may be a genius, but he's a predictable one," she replied and straightened.

Harlan looked at Jackson and grinned with boyish delight. "She called me a genius," he announced then slyly raised his brows. "She loves me."

"Yeah, I know," Jackson muttered. "You're one lucky bastard, Harlan."

Harlan's look turned serious. "Are you the commander?"

"Me? No, I'm Jackson."

"Do I know you?"

"Yeah, of course," Jackson replied. "We're comrades, and we've been friends for years."

Harlan removed his pen and wrote something on his cast. Jackson strained to see what he was writing. It simply read, 'Jackson; pretty boy; friends.' Jackson chuckled and looked at Indy across from them.

"He thinks I'm a pretty boy." Jackson again eyed the cast and read another phrase. "Wil-E-Coyote; super genius; poison," he said aloud then gave Harlan a strange look. "Okay--?"

Harlan's look was serious as he stared at Jackson. "The coyote is evil."

Jackson and Indy exchanged looks and knowing smiles. His fascination with old-time cartoons was somewhat endearing.

†

Within an hour, Flynn, Nate, and Jackson were already carrying boxes containing Liz's clothes and personal belongings down the stairs and into her awaiting car. Kale arrived a few minutes later to join the precession of movers. He brought the hearse so they wouldn't have to return for a second trip. Kale was unusually quiet from the time he arrived and didn't speak to anyone, including Indy. Indy felt uncomfortable around Kale and Liz. She knew she was partly to blame for her father's breakup and was almost certain Liz and Kale blamed her just a little too. Since there were already enough movers, Indy remained silently out of the way toward the back of the foyer near the back hallway. It pained her to see the saddened looks on the faces of Liz and her father as they carried boxes down the stairs and outside, but she wasn't sad enough to trade Harlan.

"Did something happen?" Harlan spoke from behind her.

Indy jumped with surprise and turned to see Harlan standing behind her while watching the men with boxes. She eyed him suspiciously and wondered how he had managed to sneak up on her so quietly with a cast on his leg. She attempted to relax and insecurely folded her arms across her chest, rubbing her shoulders subconsciously.

"The commander's girlfriend is moving out," Indy gently informed him.

Harlan watched in silence a moment then glanced at his cast. He looked back into the foyer beyond Indy. "The bald man?"

"Yes, he's the commander," Indy replied.

"Is that his girlfriend?" he asked while casually indicating Liz, who glanced at them before heading out the door with the last of her personal belongings.

"Yes, that's Liz."

"She doesn't like me," Harlan announced.

"I'm sure that's not true," Indy replied without looking at him. She didn't want him to look into her eyes and possibly notice she was lying to him.

"Then why did she look at me that way?" Harlan asked. "You saw the way she looked at me."

Indy turned to face him and offered a pleasant smile. "I think that look may have been directed at me," she replied. "Let's just forget about Liz and move on."

Harlan stared into Indy's eyes. She stared back and felt a dull ache sweep through her body. Last night was still fresh in her mind, yet Harlan had no idea they'd made love. She could almost feel his hands traveling her naked body. The phantom sensation was almost enough to send her body into spasms of ecstasy. Indy pushed her feelings aside and attempted to keep a level head.

"Would you like to help me prepare Christmas dinner?" she asked almost timidly.

Harlan's smile brightened. "It's Christmas?"

She felt the tears welling up in her eyes. Indy wished he'd retain some small memories throughout the day and give her some hope for his recovery. She managed a smile.

"Yes, it's Christmas Day," she replied gently. "You kissed me under the mistletoe last night."

His eyes suddenly lit up. "I did?"

Indy nodded. His boyish delight was endearing. Harlan then looked up and spotted the mistletoe above them. He grinned and pointed to it.

"Do I get a do over?"

She contained her humor to his innocent way of asking then took a step closer to him and gently touched his face. Indy placed her lips to his, hesitated a moment, and then kissed him warmly but quickly on the lips. She pulled away before he could return the kiss or make an attempt to place his arms around her. That small kiss was all she could handle at the moment, and even that was enough to send a tingling sensation throughout her body. Harlan maintained his grin and gently brushed his fingers along her cheek. Indy knew she had to put some distance between them before her body reacted in an unacceptable manner. She took his fingers and guided him toward the kitchen. Harlan reached back with his free hand when she wasn't looking and snatched the mistletoe from the archway. He happily followed her into the kitchen.

Chapter Twenty-two

Present wrappings and bows lie scattered around the family room floor not far from the large Evergreen tree lavishly decorated in gold and pink. Indy, Harlan, Flynn, Jackson, and Nate sat in their respective chairs near the Christmas tree with their newly unwrapped treasures and traditional gag gifts. Flynn and Jackson were dressed festively with Santa hats firmly planted on their heads. Nate had a candy cane sticking out of his mouth and occasionally bobbed it around as if were a cigar. Flynn's study was the only room in the house where smoking cigars was permitted. It had been Nala's rule from the day they bought the house, and the rule would remain in effect until Flynn's dying day. Indy was grateful for her father's respect toward her mother's wishes even after her death. Of course, Indy wasn't exactly fond of cigar smoke either, so that may have had something to do with it.

"Well," Flynn announced with a humored smile, "this has been a very interesting Christmas."

"Reminds me of that Christmas we'd spent in Iraq," Nate remarked.

All three men chuckled. Harlan stared at them with confusion. It was obvious he was desperate to be let in on the joke. Flynn noted his friend's bewildered stare and obliged.

"We hung mistletoe from our assault rifles," Flynn informed Harlan.

Harlan continued to stare at them as if not fully understanding the humor but found his own way of feeling included in the conversation.

"I kissed Nala under the mistletoe," Harlan announced.

Flynn frowned in response. "Yeah, I heard. Don't tell the commander," her father remarked then looked at Jackson, who sat across from him. "When he's back to himself, remind me to hit him."

Jackson gave Flynn a thumbs up. Nate suddenly chuckled and rotated the candy cane in his mouth, pinching it between his teeth on the side.

"Remember that Christmas when Harlan wrapped the bomb in holiday paper and a big red bow?" Nate remarked, barely containing his humor.

There was another round of laughter. Harlan continued to stare at the men then drifted out a moment.

"18-6-24-3-10-15," Harlan suddenly announced.

All four fell silent and stared at Harlan. Their expressions were equally stunned.

"Was that the detonation code?" Jackson suddenly asked with surprise.

Harlan's eyes became fixated on the arm of the chair. He was off in another world. "It won't detonate," Harlan announced. "I need to manually detonate it."

Harlan's thumb subconsciously pressed into the arm of the chair. Everyone stared at him in silence before sadness overtook them. It was obviously a chilling reminder of the incident that nearly claimed his life. Indy quickly jumped up from her position on the sofa and approached Harlan. She held his fingers in her hand and sat on the arm of the chair alongside him. He suddenly snapped out of his trance, looked up at her, and smiled.

"Is it bath time?"

Nate and Jackson hid their smirks while chuckling softly. Flynn just glared his annoyance at Harlan. Indy was certain her father was showing an enormous amount of restraint where his friend was concerned.

"I dug out some old photo albums," Indy informed Harlan, swiftly changing the subject. "I thought you and I could look at them tonight over hot chocolate and cookies."

Harlan grinned boyishly and caressed her hand with his fingers. "Okay."

Indy looked at her father and raised her brows. "Don't worry about us, Dad," she announced. "I know what you boys want to do tonight."

All three men exchanged looks and grinned at the silent suggestion. Flynn then appeared apprehensive while studying his daughter.

"Are you sure you don't want us to stay with you and Harlan?" Flynn asked then smiled timidly. "It is Christmas Day."

"Don't worry," she remarked. "Margo, Kale, and Roman are coming over for dinner. We don't need a bunch of hard ass soldiers ruining our good time."

Flynn suddenly grinned and chuckled. "You really are the son I'd always wanted," he announced then looked at Nate and Jackson. "We bug out in ten. Move it out, men!"

All three sprang to their feet with a little too much enthusiasm. Harlan attempted to stand but was limited by the cast on his leg and struggled to get out of the plush chair.

Indy held him back with a hand to his shoulder and a firm stare. "Sorry, soldier. You're sitting this one out."

"We're going to kick ass!" Nate said excitedly.

All three hurried from the room.

Harlan appeared concerned as he watched the men jogging from the safety of the family room. He looked at Indy with a strange expression on his face.

"What if they need me?" he suddenly asked.

"I don't think they'll need anything blown up at the paintball field."

†

Only ten minutes had passed before Flynn, Jackson, and Nate hurried down the staircase and into the foyer with their duffel bags firmly in hand. All three grinned like schoolboys. Indy approached them from the family room and admired their enthusiasm. She often wondered if they were that overzealous in the field where it really mattered. She'd never seen her father or his team in real combat before--not even pretend combat at the paintball field. She was sure they were magnificent. Flynn awaited her approach and placed his arm firmly around her shoulder.

"Are you sure you don't mind?" her father asked with sincerity in his eyes.

"Mind?" she scoffed. "You're doing me a favor by getting out of my hair." She smiled warmly. "Go, have fun. Pulverize the other teams."

"We always do," Jackson replied while raising his brows suggestively. He then hesitated and his smile faded slightly. "Though it won't be as climactic without Harlan."

"Yeah, it's not nearly as much fun if no one pisses their pants from his surprise assaults," Nate remarked.

"I'm sure he'll be back to scaring the piss out of college kids on holiday break soon enough," Indy informed them. "He's not even aware what he's missing. Don't worry about him. We're going to have the sort of fun he can have within his limitations."

Flynn smiled and kissed Indy on the forehead. "If you have any trouble--"

"We'll be fine," she interrupted. "Just go."

It didn't take much encouragement to send the three men running from the house.

Chapter Twenty-three

Margo, Kale, and Roman had joined Indy and Harlan for dinner and an evening of hanging out together. It was already a little after eight o'clock that night. Indy and her friends drank and had a good time recounting Christmas' past. Harlan sat in his overstuffed chair with his leg elevated and attentively paged through the photo album on his lap. He stopped on one of the pages and stared at it with a strange look on his face. Something had caught his attention, alerting the others. Roman appeared curious and approached.

"What did you find?" Roman asked and looked over his shoulder at the album.

Harlan pointed to a woman standing alongside him in the photo. It was Maureen. "Who's that?" he almost demanded as if something had clicked in his mind.

Roman suddenly tensed to the question, cast a quick glance at Indy, and then looked back at Harlan. "That's Maureen."

All eyes were now on Harlan as they stared in silence and awaited a response, since he'd clearly recognized her. Harlan suddenly threw the album across the floor, startling everyone. He appeared hostile while deep in thought. Indy became concerned and slowly stood. He didn't remember his wife, and he certainly didn't know she'd filed for divorce, so his sudden agitation was surprising and almost unfounded.

"Are you okay?" she gently asked.

"No," he grumbled without looking at her. He stared at the discarded album on the floor. "I'd like to go to bed now."

Indy quickly stood and approached. His eyes suddenly locked on her. He pointed a warning finger with an expression that stopped her in her tracks.

"No, you just stay away from me."

Everyone was stunned by the harsh comment but none more than Indy. Harlan looked at Roman, who stood near him.

"Will you help me?"

Roman uncertainly nodded and helped Harlan from the chair. He didn't require any assistance this time and hobbled on his cast from the room. Roman hurried after him. Indy, Margo, and Kale watched them leave with matching stares.

"What was that all about?" Margo asked softly.

"I'm not sure," Indy said gently, wondering the same thing herself. She returned to her seat while deep in thought. "Maureen filed for divorce, but I'm sure no one told him. Something must have clicked."

"But why was he angry with you?" Kale suddenly asked.

Indy shook her head, although her thoughts strayed to last night and what they'd done. She hoped his hostility toward her didn't have anything to do with what happened between them coupled with the realization that he was, at least in his mind, happily married to another woman.

"I'm not really sure," Indy replied while lost in her own guilty thoughts.

"I don't like his behavior, Indy," Kale boldly remarked and jolted her from her trance. "You saw what happened at the party with Liz. What if he vents on you next?"

She couldn't even look at Kale while her head was filled with last night. "He's not going to hurt me, Kale."

"Would you have suspected he'd hurt Liz or that nurse?" Kale suddenly asked.

"He does have a point," Margo gently announced. "He even hit Jackson."

Indy returned to her current reality and looked at Margo. "That doesn't count. He hits Jackson all the time."

"This isn't a joke, Indy," Kale informed her while becoming anxious. "The man is highly skilled on ways to kill people. What if he loses it on you?"

"He's improving," she announced. "I can handle him. Now let's just drop the subject."

Despite her own words, Indy couldn't get Harlan's hostility toward her out of her mind. His actions were concerning, allowing her guilty feelings to surface once again.

†

Two hours had passed since Roman took Harlan to his room to help him change for bed. Indy, Kale, and Margo were playing a board game, although Indy was too distracted to enjoy her friends' company. She wanted to check on Roman and Harlan, but the door was locked. Rather than knock, she left them alone, fearing she'd further upset Harlan. Her concerns over Harlan's emotional state were getting the best of her. Roman finally returned to the living room, collapsed into his chair with a look of exhaustion, and reclaimed his drink. Her friend appeared distracted and a little intent on downing his drink in record time. Indy studied him a moment and wondered what had transpired between the two of them in Harlan's room.

"Everything okay?" Indy asked with concern in her tone. "What took you so long? And why was the door locked?"

Margo faked a concerned look while hiding her grin. "He didn't make you give him a sponge bath, did he?"

"No," Roman snapped hotly. "I didn't give him a sponge bath. He just wanted to talk without any interruptions."

"Really?" Indy asked with some surprise. "What does a man with no memory want to talk about?"

Roman shifted uncomfortably in his chair. "He wanted to talk about Maureen, so I told him."

She was a little stunned that Harlan wanted to discuss a woman he didn't even remember. There had to be something more Roman wasn't telling her.

"Was he okay?" Indy asked almost timidly.

"If you define fifteen minutes of turning the television on and off while complaining that it won't detonate as okay, yeah he was okay."

"Maybe I should check on him," Indy announced and started to stand.

"He's fine," Roman muttered and cast an odd glare at her. "I think he needs to be by himself."

His comment surprised her. It was almost as if he knew something he wasn't willing to share.

"Yeah, but--"

Roman glared at her and snarled, "Just leave him alone, Indy. He's been through enough."

All three stared at Roman with surprise. Roman avoided looking at them, sipped his drink, and stared off at nothing in particular. Indy slowly returned to her seat and attempted to search for an explanation. Harlan had to have remembered last night. He remembered, and he was angry with her. Roman was attempting to protect her feelings. She resisted the temptation to talk to Harlan. She needed to listen to her friend and just leave him alone for a little while, even if it was eating her up inside.

†

Midnight was indicated by the chiming of the large grandfather clock in the foyer. Indy thought she heard a car door from outside and entered the foyer from the family room. The front door opened to reveal Flynn, Jackson, and Nate returning from their lengthy game, undoubtedly followed by a few hours at a local bar. All three were more than likely intoxicated, indicated by their laughing as they entered. Her father saw her and attempted to put on a sober appearance for her benefit.

"Oh, honey," he announced louder than he intended. "We didn't wake you, did we?"

"No, I was just going to check on Harlan then go to bed," she replied. "FYI. Roman and Kale are sleeping it off in the family room, and Margo took my bed."

"Where are you sleeping?" her father asked.

"With Margo?" Jackson asked as a devious smile crossed his face, which was then followed by a snicker.

Flynn backhanded him in the abdomen without even looking back to line up his shot. Jackson rubbed his abdomen while groaning softly.

"No," Indy snarled at Jackson. "I'll sleep on the sofa in the study."

"No, I'll take the sofa," Flynn announced. "You take my bedroom."

"I'll take the sofa," Jackson offered. "She can have my guest bedroom upstairs."

"You three work it out," Nate announced without care and headed up the stairs. "I'm going to bed."

Jackson and Flynn watched Nate climb the stairs while never once looking back.

"There goes the last of the true gentlemen," Jackson muttered under his breath.

"I'm fine with the sofa," Indy informed them. "I'm shorter. I fit better than either of you. Don't worry about it."

"If you insist," Flynn finally gave in, appearing exhausted from their night out. "How was Harlan tonight?"

Indy frowned in response while insecurely crossing her arms over her chest. "Not good," she replied gently. "He remembered Maureen, so Roman told him everything."

"Oh, God," Flynn muttered while shaking his head. "Do you think he'll remember in the morning?"

"That depends on whether or not he wrote it on his cast," Indy replied.

Flynn continued to shake his head, unable to mask the disappointment and hostility on his face. "I wish he'd listened to me about getting that prenup," he muttered. "Now he'll probably lose everything his parents left him."

Flynn patted Indy on the shoulder and headed up the stairs with less enthusiasm. Jackson frowned then looked back at Indy as if feeling his commander's pain.

"You know," Jackson announced drunkenly, "I was so close to stopping that wedding, but I just couldn't bring myself to break Harlan's heart like that."

"You wanted to stop the wedding?" Indy asked with surprise. "Why?"

It was the first time she'd heard anyone complain about Maureen or her union to Harlan. Then again, they were both drunk and not thinking clearly.

"Not all women are equipped to marry soldiers," Jackson informed her. "Maureen should have married a dentist or a lawyer. Someone who could afford the lifestyle she wanted."

"I don't get it," Indy remarked while attempting to rationalize Maureen's thinking. "She knew he wasn't rich. Why would she want to marry him?"

"She got great odds."

Indy stared at him without understanding. She wasn't sure what that was supposed to mean. Jackson placed his arm around her shoulder and walked with her to the base of the stairs. She was aware that he was basically using her as a crutch in his drunken condition.

"High mortality rate; big insurance policy," Jackson replied. "You do the math."

"You think she was hoping he'd be killed in combat?" she suddenly gasped, not grasping the concept of anyone wanting to do that to someone as adorable as Harlan.

"She'd stand to gain a million dollars in insurance alone," he replied. "That's not including his pension and other death benefits. She'd be set for life."

"Please tell me you're joking," Indy gasped softly.

Jackson offered a tiny smirk and shrugged. He kissed her quickly on the cheek.

"Night, Indy."

Chapter Twenty-four

Early the following morning, there was a firm knock on the front door. The overzealous use of the brass knocker immediately announced who was outside the door, at least to those living within the Stryker home. Indy hurried down the staircase. She was obviously fresh from the shower with her hair still damp and unkempt. Indy opened the front door to reveal a stately police officer in his early fifties, Sheriff Lerner. The sheriff was a stern, intimidating looking man with a prominent scar on his left cheek. Despite being rumored it was from a scuffle with his seven-year-old cousin when they were in the second grade, the scar commanded respect from the town's citizens.

"Morning, Indy," Sheriff Lerner announced in his most pleasant, gruff tone.

Most people believed the sheriff was an unpleasant, surly man, but Indy knew his gruff tone was little more than a façade. She'd met plenty like him over the years in the military. That he'd never been a soldier was almost surprising.

"Morning, Sheriff," she announced and offered her customary smile while greeting Sheriff Lerner.

A hint of a smile crossed his face, although it immediately disappeared. He hated showing emotion, but she always managed to drag a little out of him just to remind him that he had them. He gently cleared his throat and again turned official, which normally wasn't suspicious, but he seemed more distracted than usual.

"Sorry to bother you so early the day after Christmas, but we have a little problem on your road," he informed her. "We found a dead girl in the swamp."

The news nearly stunned Indy. Had she heard him correctly? "What?"

"Since it's just your house and the mortuary on this road, I thought maybe your father could have a look at her," Sheriff Lerner informed her. "She's not from around here, or I would have recognized her, and she had no identification. Between us, I think she was murdered."

"Murdered?" Indy gasped and stared at him a moment almost uncertain how to respond. "I don't think we've ever had a murder around here before."

"No, we haven't," he proudly announced, as if the low crime rate was due to his effectiveness as sheriff. "Unofficially, it appears as if her neck was broken."

Indy suddenly felt a cold chill run down her spine as she stared at the sheriff. A horrible thought struck her.

"Nate's girlfriend was here on Christmas Eve," she informed him with concern. "She left early Christmas morning before the others were out of bed. I hope it wasn't her."

"Twenty-something; looks to be a blonde. I'm guessing she was quite attractive," he announced. "Sort of hard to tell with the condition we found her."

Further concern swept over Indy. "You just described Nate's girlfriend," Indy announced in a slight gasp. She felt a sense of urgency to find out if the dead woman was, in fact, Nate's girlfriend. "The guys are still sleeping it off. Maybe I'd better go with you to identify the woman."

He nodded and stepped aside, allowing her to exit first. Indy was concerned over the dead woman they'd found so close to her home. What if the murdered woman was Nate's girlfriend? Who'd want to kill her? Was it a carjacking gone bad? Who'd attempt a carjacking on a deserted back road? Even though Nate's girlfriend was technically just a 'girl in port' to him, he'd still be upset by the news, and it was never good to upset Nate.

†

The coroner's wagon and several police cars were parked alongside the deserted back road. It seemed Sheriff Lerner called in every officer on their roster for their first murder since the town had been established. As Indy got out of the sheriff's cruiser, she could see a police officer taping off the entire swamp with yellow police line. As they got closer, Indy could see the empty body bag on the ground, although she didn't see the body. The coroner, a man who looked more like a country vet, squatted alongside the body bag beyond the yellow tape. Sheriff Lerner and Indy approached the coroner from behind. Indy then saw the body on the other side of the body bag. The once attractive woman wearing black pants and a mud stained, white tank top was slightly bloated and showed signs of rigor mortis. As Indy stared in shock at the condition of the woman, the reality of who she was suddenly hit her.

"Oh, my God," Indy gasped with alarm. "That's the visiting nurse."

Sheriff Lerner looked at her with moderate confusion. "The what?"

"The nurse who came out to care for Harlan when we first brought him home," Indy informed him, unable to take her eyes off the dead woman. Although she recognized the nurse, decomposition almost kept her from identifying the woman. "She quit almost a week ago."

"Our girl's only been dead twelve or so hours," the coroner offered as he stared at them and straightened.

Indy immediately made a face and couldn't take her eyes off the woman's condition. She looked to be dead days not hours. Her condition was truly unsettling.

"She reported back to the agency after she'd left. We hadn't seen her since," Indy announced then spun toward the sheriff and gave him a curious look. "Wait. That means she was killed around eight o'clock last night. That doesn't make any sense. What was she doing out here last night?"

"Good question," the sheriff remarked and raised his brows. "Just to cover our asses, can you account for the folks at your place from about--?"

Sheriff Lerner eyed the coroner.

"Between seven and ten o'clock last night," the coroner replied to the silent question.

Sheriff Lerner looked back at Indy and awaited a response. It was the first time his look sent a chill through her. She was positive he'd never accuse her father of something like murder. Her mind immediately strayed to Harlan's altercation with the nurse during her first and only visit. Indy had never been so thankful for Harlan's ironclad alibi. She attempted to remain composed, despite her initial thoughts.

"Well, my father, Jackson, and Nate were together at that paintball place, probably pulverizing their opponents," Indy informed him. "Kale, Roman, Margo, Harlan, and I were at the house together all evening. We weren't out of one another's sight for longer than ten minutes from dinnertime until around midnight. They're all still sleeping it off at my house."

"I guess that explains why Roman didn't answer his phone this morning," Sheriff Lerner muttered. He stared at Indy, again with a coldness she'd never seen before. "I heard some scuttlebutt that the injured man, Harlan, is a bit psychotic."

"He's not psychotic," she snapped hotly, immediately wishing she'd responded with less hostility. She didn't know why she was so defensive. Harlan couldn't have done it. "He was in a coma and suffers from severe memory loss. He doesn't even know his own name without being reminded."

Sheriff Lerner remained motionless with his eyes fixed on her. "I heard he attacked your father's girlfriend."

Indy wished he'd stop staring at her that way, and she didn't appreciate what he was insinuating. She didn't know why his look was sending fear through her.

"He knocked a drink from her hand. That's hardly an attack," she scoffed and folded her arms across her chest, a defense mechanism she wished she hadn't done. "I assure you, he wasn't alone for more than ten minutes last night, and he'd hardly be capable of carrying or dragging a body half a mile from the house. He has two broken arms, a broken leg, and several broken ribs. He can barely walk on his own."

"So you're positive he wasn't alone and could not have moved a body?"

"Absolutely," she replied.

The sheriff slowly relaxed his stance and seemed less threatening. Apparently, he was stepping out of the role of 'bad cop'.

"He was with the four of us until around eight when Roman helped him get ready for bed," Indy announced. "Apparently, they had some sort of guy talk until well after ten."

"Roman was with him, huh?" he announced then grinned with what Indy could only describe as relief that he wouldn't have to arrest her father's friend. "Thank God for airtight alibis. Makes my life a lot easier." He drew a deep breath and looked back at the dead woman as the coroner and his assistant picked her up and placed her inside the body bag. Sheriff Lerner looked back at Indy. "I'll let you know what we find after the autopsy. I'll have one of the guys give you a ride home."

"Thanks, Sheriff."

Chapter Twenty-five

Later that morning, Indy entered Harlan's room and found him sitting up in bed while watching cartoons with a fixed expression on his solemn face. He obviously wasn't watching the cartoon, but instead he was off in whatever world he frequented. Indy approached the bed and studied his transfixed stare at the television. He didn't even seem to notice she had entered or approached his bed. She felt some apprehension after his mood from last night, particularly regarding her. There was an excellent chance he wouldn't remember any of it, but it still troubled her that his hostility seemed to have been directed at her. She stood over his bed with no reaction or acknowledgment to her presence.

"Harlan?"

Harlan snapped out of his trance, looked at her, and immediately smiled. "I was wondering where you were."

"I had a few things to take care of this morning," she informed him, although she wasn't going to mention that those things involved identifying a dead woman.

Indy was relieved that whatever had him upset with her from last night had already left his mind. She wasn't sure why it bothered her as much as it did. It obviously had more to do with Maureen, but she still felt some guilt over what happened between them, which was mostly on her.

"We need to get you washed and dressed before breakfast," Indy announced.

Harlan's expression was priceless. "Oh, bath time," he gleefully announced.

He removed his shirt, not letting his casts slow him any, and grinned boyishly at her. Indy couldn't resist smiling and shook her head at his childlike fascination. Jackson had been right; Harlan by all accounts should have been dead. If he got some perverse pleasure from bath time, it didn't matter. He was alive. Her attention shifted to his left cast. She sat on the bed and examined the new markings. Several areas were blackened out with permanent marker, including the area referencing her sexually. Had Roman lied? Was Harlan more upset than he led on?

"What happened here?" she asked of the markings on his left arm cast.

"I have no idea. I've been trying to figure that out all morning," he replied and studied the blacked areas with great interest. "Looks like something had been scratched out and then colored over." He gave her a puzzled look. "Who'd do something like that?"

Indy wasn't sure she liked the behavior he had been displaying and would need to question Roman further on what Harlan had been doing last night. She studied the blackened areas a little closer. Harlan had been correct. There were scratches beneath the permanent marker, removing any trace of what had been written beneath it. Indy's thoughts immediately strayed to the photo album and Harlan's outburst directed toward her. She couldn't fight the feelings any longer and stared into Harlan's eyes.

"Were you mad at me last night?" Indy blurted out and almost immediately regretted it.

Harlan stared back at her and seemed puzzled. "I don't think so. You give me my bath." He grinned proudly. "I could never be mad at you."

She wanted to believe him, but his mood last night was evidence enough to tell a different story. Indy again studied the scratched out and blackened areas with concern. She was almost relieved that the one referencing her was gone. She inhaled deeply then offered a warm smile.

"Well, maybe certain reminders are best left hidden," she remarked.

"I wouldn't be able to remember your name if it wasn't written on my cast," he contradicted, obviously not caring for her opinion. "Could I have a tablet? I seem to have run out of space on my casts."

She had to admit, he did a fantastic job of filling all the available space on both his casts. Left-handed writing wasn't a hindrance for the man of many talents. In the past, he boasted being able to read upside down, which didn't surprise her. Harlan was a man who'd never forgotten anything that had happened in his life. His memory was astounding, which is what made his current situation all the more saddening.

"I'll see if I can find one for you."

†

Morning had passed quickly and it was nearly noon. Roman was the first to rise and seemed in a hurry to leave despite his hangover. Indy saw him attempting to make an escape and hurried onto the porch after him. He had to have seen her, but he didn't stop. She caught up to him before he reached the steps and grabbed his arm. He was hesitant to stop, judging by the amount of pressure she was forced to use on his arm. He turned to face her and immediately ran his fingers through his hair. Judging by his condition, his hangover was massive.

"We need to talk," Indy announced firmly.

Roman groaned softly and looked as if he were about to heave. "Can we talk later, Indy?" he questioned. "I'm suffering from major hangover here."

She could see that much, but she wasn't letting him go without some answers.

"No, it's important," Indy announced. "What happened last night with Harlan?"

Roman groaned and leaned heavily against the support beam, allowing his head to hit the post a little hard than intended.

"He asked about Maureen, so I told him," he announced as his eyes rolled open and met her gaze. "He got a little weird, and I tried to smooth things over."

"Was he mad at me?"

Roman suddenly straightened and appeared surprised by the question. "Mad at you? Why would he be mad at you?" he asked then hesitated as his eyes widened. "Oh, you mean because of what was written on his cast?" A strange grin crossed Roman's stubbly face. "I'm pretty sure I don't want to know what happened there, but he wasn't mad at you."

"He scratched different writings from his cast and colored them over with permanent marker," she informed him with a firmness that demanded an explanation.

"Yeah, I know," Roman replied casually. "He was doing that with a butter knife while we talked. Don't worry; I removed the butter knife before I left." His expression softened despite how poorly he must have been feeling. "You don't need to worry, Indy, he wasn't mad at you. All his anger was at Maureen." He hesitated then inhaled deeply while sinking into thought. "Then ten minutes later, he moved on to the next thing." He looked back at Indy. "It was an endless loop of anger toward Maureen, thinking the coyote was after him, bombs not detonating, and where you were with his bath."

Indy attempted to relax though it wasn't easy. "I'm glad to hear." She subconsciously ran her fingers through her hair while feeling the guilt returning. Now Roman knew what she'd done too. "I didn't mean for it to happen, Roman," she remarked timidly. "I guess I was still dealing with his near death, and when he came on to me, I just couldn't turn him down."

"Sympathy sex. I get it."

"No, I'm not sure you do," she announced then groaned. "It goes beyond sympathy. He almost died. I almost lost him. I needed that closeness."

"Yeah, I still get it. Comfort sex."

Indy sighed, allowing her arms to fall to her sides. "Close enough."

"So what now?" Roman questioned, appearing alert to the prospect of a sexual conversation. "Are you going to continue servicing him?"

She glared at her friend. She loved Roman dearly, but he could be a pervert at times.

"Not that I don't appreciate your crudeness, but, no, it's over," she announced bluntly then felt slightly insecure about the entire incident. "He doesn't remember any of it, and the writing is no longer on the wall...so to speak."

"That's for the best," Roman replied with less enthusiasm. "You're like a niece to him, and knowing he slept with you is liable to kill him." He inhaled deeply and again looked as if he was about to heave. "He has enough problems without living with that sort of guilt. Not to mention your father would kill him if he ever found out."

Indy was very aware of the consequences if that happened, and she trusted Roman not to say anything. He liked Harlan and didn't want to see anything bad happen to him either.

"I'm feeling guilty enough for both of us," Indy announced gently. "I'd prefer it if that memory never returned to him."

Roman straightened. "Can I go now? I really don't feel--" Before he could even finish the sentence, he turned toward the railing and vomited over the side and into the bushes.

"Okay, I think we're finished here," Indy announced while grimacing.

She turned and hurried back into the house. If she had to see, hear, or smell any more of that, she'd be doubled over the railing alongside him.

Chapter Twenty-six

Two days later, Indy and Harlan sat at the kitchen table with a bored game between them and a plate full of Christmas cookies. Harlan ate a cookie as he rolled the die then moved his play piece the appropriate amount of spaces. He picked up the card, read it, and groaned.

"I keep going back to the bog," Harlan protested then moved his piece back to the undesired location. He frowned his disapproval and pointed at the board. "That place is a hellhole. Last time I was there, someone jumped me from behind and nearly tore off my testicles."

Indy looked at Harlan with surprise by the comment. She didn't know what game he was playing, but she didn't remember Candyland being that violent. Their game was interrupted by someone knocking on the front door. Harlan immediately looked around with concern.

"Did you hear that?" he suddenly asked.

"Yes, someone's at the front door," she replied while standing. "I'll see who's at the door. You just sit in the bog and watch out for marauders."

"Oh, I will," he announced firmly.

Indy eyed him with concern then hurried from the kitchen. She crossed the foyer and approached the front door. Utilizing the peek hole was not something she'd ever done in the past, since nothing ever happened in their small town. That was, until the visiting nurse was murdered. Indy opened the door and stared at Maureen standing in the doorway. Indy's heart nearly pounded through her chest at the sight of Harlan's soon-to-be ex-wife. There was a time when she was happy to see the woman, but those feelings were replaced with anger and hostility. Despite Maureen's timid smile, Indy gripped the doorknob and sneered at the woman.

"What do you want?" Indy demanded.

Maureen appeared surprised by the tone and equally scathing words from Indy. She blinked several times as her lips parted slightly.

"I came to see Harlan," she announced almost innocently, as if it were a common occurrence.

Indy released the doorknob and leaned her shoulder against the doorframe while folding her arms across her chest. Her expression was cold.

"I think it was made perfectly clear that you only speak to Harlan through his lawyer," Indy scoffed.

"He's my husband," Maureen firmly protested, her innocent appearance quickly turning angry and hostile. "I can see him if I want to."

"No, you can't," Indy hissed back. "Anything you have to say, you'll need to say to his lawyer. He doesn't remember you, and it's in his best interest that he has no contact with you until the divorce is final." Indy's eyes narrowed as she glared at the woman. "And even then, I'm not letting you anywhere near him."

"I'm withdrawing the divorce," Maureen announced while holding her head up high. "I want to see my husband. In fact, I'm petitioning to have him moved back into our house."

Indy felt her entire body twitch at the words. Her heart pounded rapidly as fright swept through her. She couldn't do that! Could she?

"Now get out of my way," Maureen snapped and shoved past Indy into the foyer.

Indy was momentarily thrown off balance then turned and watched Maureen strut into her house. She looked around for Harlan while making her way along the foyer. Indy bolted after her, grabbed her by the arm, and slung her backward, forcing her to face her. Indy's look was wild and unpredictable.

"Get out of my house!"

"I'm taking Harlan home with me," Maureen blurted out, "and there's nothing you can do to stop me!"

She attempted to storm past Indy. Indy suddenly kicked her in the abdomen. As she doubled over, she punched her in the mouth, sending her to the floor. Indy sneered and stood over the writhing woman.

"You can either walk out or be carried out," Indy snarled in a hateful tone.

Maureen suddenly kicked Indy in the shin, nearly catching her in the knee. Indy fell to the floor with a thump that sent pain through her hip. Maureen jumped on top of her and screamed while punching her in the face. She coiled back for a second punch, which Indy prepared to block. Maureen suddenly cried out as she was pulled off Indy by a casted arm around her waist. Harlan tossed Maureen across the foyer floor with such force that she slid in circles across the hardwood. Harlan stood defensively in front of Indy and glared at Maureen on the floor several feet away. Maureen stared at the cold expression on Harlan's face as his eyes cut through her. She slowly stood while facing him. Indy sprang to her feet and attempted to bolt past Harlan. He extended his casted arm, stopping her, and forced her to remain behind him.

"Harlan," Maureen announced with a soft gasp while staring at him. "It's me, Maureen, your wife. Remember?" She smiled sweetly and attempted to charm him with her bedroom eyes. "I'm here to take you home, away from these people. They've been trying to keep us apart."

"You lying bitch," Indy growled and again attempted to bolt past Harlan.

Harlan caught her arm and nearly slung her back to her position behind him. His eyes remained locked on Maureen with a look of mayhem on his face.

"I don't care who you are," Harlan boldly announced. "This is my home, and I'm not going anywhere with you. And if you ever touch Indy again, you'll regret it."

"But, Harlan--" Maureen protested.

"Get out," he growled lowly and pointed to the door. "And don't ever come back."

Maureen stared at him and appeared frightened for the first time. She quickly grabbed her discarded purse and hurried from the house, slamming the front door behind her. Harlan turned to face Indy. His look immediately softened as he gently touched the red mark on her face.

"Are you okay?"

Indy stared at Harlan with surprise. "You remembered my name."

"Yes," he replied. "Can we finish our game now? There are some pretty seedy characters in that bog, but I can't get out until my next turn. I fear they may torture me soon."

Indy attempted to hide her smile. She didn't care how insane he sounded, she was just happy he remembered her name without consulting his cast for once. The front door was suddenly thrown open with a thunderous crack, startling both. Harlan spun on his cast so fast that he nearly fell to the floor. Flynn entered the foyer and looked at them with alarm.

"Was that Maureen who nearly ran me down in my own driveway?" Flynn demanded.

"Yeah," Indy remarked with disgust. "She's petitioning to have Harlan returned home. She claims she changed her mind about the divorce."

"I'll bet she has," Flynn announced then snorted a laugh. "Harlan's lawyer discovered she had signed a prenuptial agreement prior to their getting married. If she divorces him, she gets nothing. Her lawyer probably told her that this afternoon." He grinned his pleasure. "Harlan's lawyer is going to proceed with the divorce on his behalf. Maureen gets nothing except some furniture and her personal belongings."

"That's wonderful," Indy announced while breathing a sigh of relief. She looked at Harlan, who had no idea what they were even talking about. "You're free, Harlan."

"Really?" he announced with surprise. "So it's my turn to roll then?"

Indy held back her laugh. "Yeah, it's your turn to roll. Let's finish that game."

Harlan appeared pleased and hurried as fast as his cast would allow him to travel back to the kitchen. Indy smiled at her father and followed Harlan.

Chapter Twenty-seven

Just three days after the New Year, Indy, Jackson, Harlan, and Flynn sat at a booth at the local diner. The diner was particularly busy that morning, being the town was returning to a sense of normalcy after the holiday season had finally ended. Harlan sat alongside Indy while picking at his French fries and subconsciously rubbed his bare arms. The casts had finally been removed, leaving his arms a little paler in comparison to the rest of his body. Surprisingly, he hadn't lost much muscle tone in his lower arms. He seemed unusually preoccupied with the new sensation and was barely able to concentrate on much else than his cast free limbs. Jackson watched Harlan repeatedly rubbing his arms. It wasn't as if they all hadn't been there at one point during their tour of duty.

"How does it feel to be free from your cast hell?" Jackson asked while hiding his humored smile.

Harlan glanced at him but didn't seem to share his enthusiasm. "Like I'm naked."

Both Jackson and Flynn were amused by the response. Physically, he was in fine shape, and it wouldn't take much to return his body to a weapon of mass destruction. His mind was the continuing saga of despair.

"I bet you're dying for a good old-fashioned shower," Flynn announced then slyly eyed Indy with a knowing grin. "No more sponge baths."

Harlan sharply shifted his attention to Flynn, as the magnitude of the comment appeared to sink in. There was an odd moment of silence.

"Huh?" Harlan snorted softly in response then hesitated. "Well, that sucks."

Jackson chuckled at the remark then minded his own meal. Ending the conversation on sponge baths was in everyone's best interest. Flynn's sense of humor only went so far.

"What did the doctor say about your memory loss?" Flynn finally asked Harlan.

Harlan considered the question then flipped through his notepad, which was filled with entries. Flynn glanced at Indy for an immediate response. Her father had never been a particularly patient man when it came to answering questions.

"He wasn't concerned," Indy replied with a shrug. "He said it's only been two weeks since he came out of the coma. The doctor is encouraged that he thinks to write things down and actually remembers to consult his notepad."

Flynn sank back in his chair with a look that conveyed his distaste for the diagnosis. "But he still doesn't remember one day to the next," he protested. "That didn't concern him at all? You know, I never liked that doctor."

"Have you ever liked any doctor?" Indy inquired while raising her brow.

Flynn glared back at her. The answer was obvious. Her father didn't think neither doctors nor nurses knew what they were talking about. Even when they were right, he'd always disagree with them. It was the thickheaded commander in him.

"He's not worried just yet," Indy casually replied. "He's optimistic that he finally maintains his memory throughout the day, even if he does forget by the next morning. He believes it's encouraging."

Flynn rolled his eyes and groaned. He obviously had more to say on the subject, but Indy was just as thickheaded, so there was little point. Harlan appeared concerned about something and frantically flipped through his notepad. Indy acknowledged his reaction and eyed the notepad. There were words, sentences, paragraphs, and an equal amount of number combinations written on every page.

"Something wrong?" Indy asked Harlan, snapping him out of his frustrated page flipping.

"I'm missing a page," he announced and stared at the blank page before him. The last entry was from last night. His morning entries were missing. He aggressively tapped the blank page. "It was here. I wrote breakfast here, but it's gone."

Flynn casually eyed his comrade. "Maybe you forgot to write this morning's entry in your journal," he remarked.

"No," Harlan informed him while looking across the table and again indicated the tablet. "I wrote what I had for breakfast right here. I think the doctor took it." He suddenly looked at Indy with a look of alarm that concerned her. "Why would he take my last entry?"

"I don't think the doctor took a page from your journal, Harlan," Indy gently informed him.

Harlan didn't appear convinced and again flipped through the journal, as if the entries would suddenly reappear. He stopped on the second to last page. He was obviously upset over the missing pages with that morning's entries.

"We had leftover turkey for dinner last night," Harlan informed them. "I had a glass of white wine, and Indy had two brownies for dessert."

"I most certainly did not," Indy protested then immediately wondered how he possibly saw her snitch that second brownie. She didn't even think he was paying attention.

He continued to scan his notes. "Jackson told a joke about a prostitute walking into a bar--" Harlan began.

"Inappropriate," Jackson muttered and secretly attempted to indicate the crowded diner.

Harlan scanned more notes then indicated Flynn. "And the commander cursed out Nate for his crude remark about--"

"Also inappropriate," Flynn retorted gruffly.

Harlan wrote on his pad under the current date. Indy watched him write what he ate for lunch and a general description of the conversation. He was extremely detailed in his observations.

"We're going to need more notepads," Indy remarked to the others then studied Harlan's past entries in the journal. "You're still writing about the coyote?"

"What's with the coyote?" Jackson asked with a look of confusion on his face.

Indy looked at Jackson across the table and grinned. "The coyote is evil."

Harlan responded without even looking up from his journal, "The coyote is a super genius."

What Indy wouldn't give for a slight peek into Harlan's mind. Flynn appeared uncomfortable and picked at his food, which was unusual. His appetite was almost as good as Nate's appetite. His actions caught Indy's attention.

"What's wrong, Dad?" she finally asked. "You've been squirming in your seat since we sat down."

Harlan looked across the table, as if suddenly interested in the conversation, and then frantically flipped through his notepad.

"I saw something about his boxer shorts," Harlan boldly announced, nearly alerting the entire diner.

"My shorts are fine," Flynn muttered then looked at his daughter across from him. "I didn't know how to tell you, Indy." He again shifted in his seat as if fearing her reaction. "We're being called back."

She was alarmed by the comment and leaned across the table, nearly knocking her plate off the edge onto the floor. "You're going back out in the field?"

"Well, yes and no," he replied, attempting to sugarcoat his response. "Our prisoner from the compound is being held for interrogation, but he's not talking. They want us to go back to the compound and help sift through the rubble." He leaned back in his chair and seemed to relax. "We just need to find something that will make him talk."

"Is it dangerous?" she suddenly demanded, not buying his story. "You were nearly killed just six weeks ago."

Harlan observed the conversation and frantically wrote in his journal. He was having a hard time keeping up.

"No, it's not dangerous, dear," Flynn replied in a tone that didn't ease her tension any. "Half the compound was leveled along with most of the resistance. Our guys have been there nearly a month. The area is secure."

Indy's eyes narrowed as she glared at her father. "You're not just saying that so I won't worry, are you?"

"No, of course not," Flynn remarked and gave her a concerned look. "I'm actually more worried about you and Harlan. I'm concerned you might be overwhelmed."

As Indy stared into his eyes, she knew he was embellishing his safety, but his concerns over her caring for Harlan by herself were genuine. He certainly didn't need the added stress of worrying about her and Harlan. It was in her father's best interest if she played along and pretended she believed he wasn't putting himself in any danger by going back out to the compound.

"We'll be fine," Indy assured him. "Kale is a short drive away if we need anything, and Margo tends to stay over a lot when you're away."

It was her father's turn to study her, as if attempting to believe what she was telling him. He raised a sharp brow while staring at her.

"Are you sure you can handle everything?"

Indy slipped her arm around Harlan's arm and clung to him while smiling at her father. "We'll be fine," she announced then looked at Harlan. "Won't we?"

Harlan looked from Flynn to Indy and appeared curious. "Will I need my service pistol?"

Flynn and Jackson stared at Harlan with surprise, which quickly turned to concern.

"No," Flynn announced firmly. "We'll just keep that locked up for now."

Arming Harlan was the last thing any of them wanted. Even Indy would agree with them on that one, but she remained positive by the comment.

"Hey, at least he remembers having a service pistol," Indy remarked. "That's a good sign."

Flynn stared at Indy with a fixed expression conveying his concerns. "Why am I suddenly uncomfortable?"

Harlan quickly scanned his notepad. "I'm pretty sure that has something to do with boxer shorts--"

Chapter Twenty-eight

Four days had passed since Indy's father and the remainder of his team, namely Jackson and Nate, had announced their *non-dangerous* assignment. They had just left that morning, leaving Indy feeling slightly anxious and insecure, as she did most times when her father returned to active duty. Indy and Margo sat on the sofa within the family room and watched the lightly falling snow through the large windows. Neither woman had said a word in quite some time. Margo seemed to have a sixth sense when it came to Indy's moods. Sometimes, Indy just needed someone to be in the same room with her. Conversation between close friends wasn't always necessary, since they more or less knew what the other was thinking anyway. The sound of repetitive tapping continued non-stop, intruding on what should have been total silence. Neither woman commented on the sound even though they obviously heard it.

Indy returned from her concerns over her father's departure for 'compounds unknown' and glanced at Harlan, who sat on the overstuffed lounge chair with his new laptop computer. He appeared engrossed in it and typed enthusiastically. Indy wasn't even aware he knew how to type, let alone so fast. Earlier that day, she'd looked over his shoulder once just to make certain he was actually typing and not just hitting keys producing random letters. His endless talents never ceased to amaze her. She just wondered what was going through his mind that he needed to document endlessly. It wasn't as if there had been much of a conversation between Indy and her friend. Of course there hadn't. Neither woman wanted their every word taken down verbatim. Margo followed Indy's gaze to the covert stenographer.

"What's with Ernest Hemingway over there?" Margo finally asked.

"The commander bought him a laptop before he left this morning," Indy casually replied. "I think he's addicted to it. Thank God, he hasn't figured out the internet yet. I was hoping he'd grow tired with it by now." Indy turned her attention toward Harlan and smiled as he typed without care or even needing a second to collect his thoughts. "Enjoying your new toy?"

Harlan grinned proudly without taking his eyes from the screen or interrupting his typing. "It's fascinating."

"Are you sure he's actually writing stuff?" Margo asked softly under her breath. Her look was stern. "He's not retyping the same phrase, right? Because, if he comes after us with an ax, I'm so out of here."

Indy laughed softly at the comment. "I've taken a peek at his work. Some are random thoughts, conversations throughout the day, and the occasional rant about the coyote, but there's nothing concerning, trust me."

"Is he still day-to-day with his memory?" Margo asked.

"Day-to-day, yes, but once he reads what he's written, he retains most of it the entire day. What he remembers can be selective at times, but it's fascinating." Indy glanced at Harlan across the room. "Harlan, what was the temperature yesterday?"

Without looking up from his laptop, he replied, "Forty degrees with some sun and clouds."

"What did we have for dinner last Monday?"

"Pizza with sausage," he replied with little emotion then frowned. "I wanted anchovies, but you said no."

Margo looked back at Indy with her mouth hanging open and appeared stunned. "Oh, my God," she gasped. "Could he always do that?"

"He has an eidetic memory. He used to remember *everything*," Indy replied then looked back at Harlan. "What's the disarming code for the last bomb you detonated?"

The typing immediately stopped for the first time in over an hour, leaving the room in near silence. Harlan suddenly looked up and stared at her with surprise.

"That's classified."

Indy held back her laugh, looked at Margo, and grinned. "He's adorable."

"Yeah, in a Norman Bates sort of way," Margo replied dryly. "Does his doctor think he'll eventually remember who he is? I mean, it seems to me that something inside that head of his will have to give eventually."

"His doctor thinks it's more of a memory block than memory loss," Indy informed her. "PTS from the explosion. It could come back to him piece by piece or all at once."

Margo stared at Indy with surprise by the comment. "You mean he could wake up one morning and suddenly remember everything?" she gasped then raised her brows and snorted a soft laugh. "That could be interesting."

Although Indy didn't tell Margo about Christmas Eve, she had the nagging feeling her friend knew more than she let on. There was always the possibility that Roman said something. He could be a terrible gossip at times.

"What's this I heard about that visiting nurse?" Margo asked, changing the subject.

"That's where things get interesting," Indy announced. "The agency said they never sent anyone and had no idea who she even was. Sheriff Lerner thinks she was a professional thief using the visiting nurse ploy to access homes and easy targets." Indy shifted on the sofa and shook her head. "Can you imagine someone prowling around hospitals looking for their next victim? It's pretty disturbing, when you think about it."

"Imagine her surprise," Margo remarked then appeared humored. "Did she ever pick the wrong house."

Something about Margo's comment bothered Indy. She was right. Why would a professional thief target a veteran's hospital? The chance of a veteran owning and being willing to use a gun was far greater than casing a nursing home.

"Did you want me to stay tonight?" Margo asked.

Indy snapped out of her trance and smiled warmly. She'd never ask her friend to stay on a weeknight. It would be inconvenient for her with having to work the next day.

"No, we'll be fine," Indy announced. "You have work in the morning, and we're fifteen minutes in the opposite direction of your commute."

"Just remember, I offered," Margo remarked then stood. "If you're sure you don't want the company, I'll be heading out. I'll call you around lunchtime tomorrow and check on you."

"Thanks, Margo," Indy announced and walked with her to the family room archway before the grand foyer. "Drive carefully. Good night."

Margo waved and headed out the front door. Once the door shut, Indy turned in the archway and glanced at Harlan, who remained entertained, happily typing on his new toy.

"I'm exhausted," Indy informed him, barely breaking his concentration. "Could I convince you to work on that in your room? I'd like to turn in early."

He stopped typing and looked at her with a hint of his former arrogance. "Are you afraid I won't be able to find my room on my own?" Harlan asked.

That he poked fun at his own memory issues was encouraging. He at least knew there was a problem, which possibly meant his memory would eventually come back to him.

"We moved your room upstairs this morning, remember?" she announced and awaited his response.

Harlan's arrogance quickly vanished as he considered her earlier question with more forethought. "Maybe you should take me to my room," he suggested.

Chapter Twenty-nine

Harlan followed Indy into the upstairs bedroom that had recently been occupied by Jackson. With Harlan's leg cast off and the rest of the team gone for a few weeks, Flynn thought it was best if Harlan stayed in the room adjoining Indy's bedroom via a joint bathroom. Indy agreed it was a good idea. Harlan uncertainly looked around the much smaller guestroom decorated with a male guest in mind. He appeared bewildered while clinging to his laptop like a security blanket. His mind was obviously reeling to sort out the new information.

"This doesn't look right."

Indy immediately realized he was insecure about the room change. It was the first real change to his life since moving into the Stryker home. She needed to reassure him that the move was in his best interest and hope it didn't upset him.

"That's because we moved you this morning, remember? You haven't slept in this room yet," Indy informed him then indicated the television. "There's the T.V. The remote is on the bed." She indicated the bathroom just across the room. "And that's the bathroom you and I share. If you need me, I'm right through that door." She studied the distant look on his face as he scanned the room without moving further inside. "I'm going to leave the bathroom door open and the light on. If you need anything, you come and get me, okay?"

"Yes," he replied mechanically without looking at her and gripped his laptop under his arm.

She continued to gauge his expression and body language. He looked around the room as if expecting the boogeyman to appear from under the bed at any moment. Indy was starting to feel uncomfortable about the abrupt room change and was wishing they had done it prior to her father leaving.

"Do you need anything else before I go to bed?" she asked gently.

Harlan uncertainly looked around and responded without looking at her. "Where are you going to be?"

Indy again pointed to the open bathroom doorway even though he didn't look at her. "Through that door on the other side of the bathroom."

Harlan's anxiety appeared to rise as he continued to look around while clinging to his laptop. "This doesn't look right," he repeated with increasing concern then looked at her. "Do I have to stay here?"

Indy approached the bed, pulled the covers down, and patted it. Harlan uncertainly approached and sat on the bed. She took the laptop from him, set it aside, and handed him the remote control. He began pushing the on and off button repeatedly without even looking at the television. She already didn't like his reaction. He'd been transitioning nicely, and one little room change was about to throw him into an anxiety attack. Indy removed his shoes for him, straightened, and studied him a moment longer. He didn't look at her, but instead, stared past her while pressing the remote control button. She gently touched his face. He finally looked at her, although his actions with the remote control continued subconsciously. His look was thoroughly lost.

"Would you like me to stay and watch a movie with you?" she asked gently. It would actually make her feel better.

"I'd like that," he replied while remaining in his own, otherworld.

Indy took his hand and guided him to the armoire containing the television. She opened the bottom door to reveal dozens of movies on disk.

"You pick something and put it in the player," she informed him. "I'm going to my room and change for bed. I'll be right back."

Harlan scanned the movie titles and appeared to fade out, failing in his mission to find a suitable movie. Indy headed through the bathroom and entered her dimly lit bedroom. With only the light from the connecting bathroom filtering into her room, she approached her drawer and removed a tank top and shorts to wear for the night. Harlan appeared in the bathroom doorway and peered inside. Her back was to the bathroom, and she hadn't noticed him. He still held the remote control and pressed the button while watching Indy in silence. Indy remained unaware of his presence and proceeded to change in the dim lighting of her bedroom. She removed her shirt and bra, allowing Harlan a full side view of her breast. She slipped into her tank top and pulled her shorts overtop of her panties. As Indy turned, she saw Harlan standing in the doorway watching her. He stared at her with a strange expression on his face. She immediately knew he'd seen enough of her naked body in the dim lighting to pique his interest, but she wasn't going to react. It wasn't his fault.

"Is it bath time?" he suddenly asked as his eyes strayed across her body then returned to gaze into her eyes.

"You had your shower this morning," Indy announced while attempting to keep her reactions as close to normal as possible for Harlan's sake.

Indy approached him and attempted to usher him back to his room. He didn't turn or look away from her. His finger continued to press the remote control button with increased tension and possible agitation.

"You didn't wash me," he informed her. "You're supposed to wash me."

She realized the small interruption to what was familiar had thrown him completely off. He was regressing, and it frightened her. She was supposed to be helping him move forward; not shove him backward.

"Your casts are off," Indy reminded him. "You can wash yourself now, remember?"

He stared and initially didn't respond. It was hard to tell what was going through his head.

"I'd rather have you wash me."

She wasn't going to argue with him in his current state. He was already hanging on the edge of anxiety, and she certainly didn't want to use the sedation injection on him. Indy was certain he'd be fine. She just needed to coddle him a little tonight.

"Okay, how about this," she suggested. "I'll assist you in the shower tomorrow morning. Fair enough?"

His eyes suddenly narrowed as he stared at her. "You're sneaky," he boldly announced, seemingly coming back to life. "You think I'll forget, but I'm going to write it down."

Indy felt her body sag with relief. She laughed softly at the comment and gently touched his lower arm. "I can almost see the neurons firing in your head." She took his hand in hers and guided him back through the bathroom. "Come on; let's go write that down before you forget."

Harlan clung to her hand and obediently followed her. His finger continued to press the button on the remote control but with less vigor.

Chapter Thirty

Indy slept peacefully while curled on her side on top of the covers within Harlan's bed. A light was flashing, although it didn't disturb her sleep. Harlan sat on the bed alongside Indy and pressed the on and off button on the remote control, turning the television continually on and off. He looked at Indy as she slept on her side facing away from him and stared at her through the glow of the television. His look conveyed deep thought. He slowly set the remote aside, lay down on the bed, and nuzzled against Indy from behind. Less than an hour later, Harlan lie pressed against Indy's back while holding her as she slept. He suddenly woke, as if for no apparent reason, lifted his head, and looked around the room with disorientation. He then noticed the familiar woman in his arms. Harlan appeared moderately confused as he stared at the sleeping woman. He assessed the situation only a moment before he gently caressed her hip and thigh. Indy woke and, with little forethought, stopped his traveling hand.

"I heard something," he whispered over her shoulder and close to her ear.

The sensation of his warm breath against her ear sent shock waves through her body.

"It could be the coyote."

"The coyote isn't here," she replied in a weary tone without moving from her comfortable position against his warm body. "It's just us."

She didn't want to admit how good it felt having Harlan pressed against her, but she needed to keep herself from reacting or encouraging his lustful behavior.

"Go back to sleep," she announced gently.

"I should check," he replied softly while keeping his lips close to her ear.

Indy couldn't be sure, but she swore he purposely brushed his lips against her neck. The sensation was overwhelming and tingled throughout her body.

"Where's my service pistol?" he whispered.

Any erotic thoughts she'd been struggling to resist were immediately thwarted by his requesting his service pistol. Indy sighed softly, rolled onto her back, and looked at him through the dim glow of the television.

"You don't need your service pistol," she assured him, hoping he'd believe her.

Harlan moved onto his elbow and hovered over her with a serious look on his face. She hadn't realized how close he had been until now. He eyed her cleavage above her tank top then allowed his finger to trace the neckline while staring with fixation. Indy watched with surprise as he ran his finger along her cleavage just above her tank top. She knew she should stop his gently caressing finger while pretending it wasn't a big deal, but it was a big deal. Unfortunately, it was a big deal for the wrong reason. She desperately feared he'd do something to arouse her beyond control. Indy knew she needed to get out of Harlan's bed and resist his behavior, but she couldn't force herself to do either of those.

"I need to find the commander," Harlan gently insisted. His words came across as stern and serious, but his tone and actions were playful and seductive. "I'm sure I heard something. It might be the coyote."

A second reference to the coyote was all she needed to hear to halt her arousal. Indy gently stopped his caressing hand and offered a sympathetic smile.

"You're just hearing things," she announced gently. "Go back to sleep."

His determination to fixate on the coyote wasn't going to help him relax. She needed to work on another angle. Indy nestled against him, hoping her relaxed body against his would do the same for him. Surprisingly, it worked. Harlan held her in his arms and nuzzled against her. Her plan then immediately backfired. She felt his hand firmly caressing her hip and heard a slight groan escape his throat. Indy immediately tensed and pondered her next move. Keeping him calm *and* stopping him from probing her body was going to take some finesse--and a lot of restraint on her behalf. He nuzzled his cheek against the top of her head.

"You must really want those disarming codes--"

Her heart pounded to the comment. He was off in another world fighting some imaginary villains, and it concerned her with good reason. She needed to stay calm and not let him become worked up.

"No, just a couple hours sleep."

No reaction seemed the best decision in their current situation. Ignore the behavior and it will stop. Not exactly out of the Flynn Stryker playbook, which leaned toward 'drop and give me twenty'. His hand no longer caressed her hip. Indy was almost stunned that her way had worked. She'd be sure to gloat her success to her father later. Without warning, Harlan aggressively pulled her on top of him while simultaneously tossing himself onto his back. He swiftly placed her in a compromising position on top of him, forcing her to straddle his hips. She was moderately startled by his actions. He firmly caressed her buttocks while staring into her stunned eyes.

"You can interrogate me all you want, but you won't get those codes," he announced firmly but in a seductive tone as his hand traveled her body.

Indy was suddenly concerned about his current state of mind. She no longer knew within what world he was living. Did he even know who she was? Or did he think she was someone entirely different? She attempted to pull away from him, but she wasn't able to move. In order to get away from him, it would take physical force, and she was unwilling to go that route. Hurting him was the last thing she wanted to do, and there was also the possibility any aggression on her part would be returned. She didn't need to get into a physical altercation with Harlan. If he played for keeps, she'd never win. Indy kept her arms tense, although it didn't put much distance between them. She stared into his eyes while attempting to remain as calm as possible.

"You're not just being playful, are you?" she gasped softly then attempted to mask her concern. "You're really lost inside your own mind this time."

Harlan appeared oblivious to her words as he pulled her hips firmly against his then affectionately kissed her cleavage. The duel sensation of his hard body pressing against her crotch and the warmth of his lips against her bare chest was enough to send shock waves of desire throughout her entire body. Even if she could turn off the erotic images from Christmas Eve, she couldn't control the throbbing ache for him coming from her body. Indy shut her eyes and groaned softly. As he clutched her legs on either side of his hips, he grinded firmly and rhythmically upward against her. Her head was spinning, and all Indy could think about was shedding her clothes and allowing him unhindered access to her body.

As her sexual desire began taking control of her mind, she was reminded of the guilt she'd felt after their last incident. Indy made a conscious effort to stop him. She immediately tensed and pushed against him. He was unprepared for her sudden force and movement, and she was successfully able sit upright while still on her knees. Unfortunately, her current position straddling his hips didn't exactly help the situation. Harlan seemed particularly pleased with the move. Before she could move off him, he clutched her hips and held her straddled over him, continuing his firm yet slow thrusts against her. Her new position allowed for greater penetration of the thin clothes between them, and a new sensation flooded throughout her body. She gasped softly and immediately cursed herself for the pleasure to which she'd allowed overtake her. Indy endured the pleasurable feeling only for a moment before guilt again returned. She caught his hands clinging to her hips and successfully stopped his grinding against her. He met her gaze as if it were all part of foreplay. She inhaled deeply and smiled timidly.

"Why don't I fix you a drink while you review the notes in your laptop?"

Before he fully understood the words she'd said, Indy removed his hands from her hips, and scrambled off him. She jumped off the bed with such vigor that she nearly fell to the floor. His little seduction scene had left her moderately weak and almost dizzy with desire, if that was even possible. Harlan moved to his elbow, seductively reclined, and watched her with a lustful grin across his face.

"Will you finish interrogating me later?"

Indy looked at him with some surprise while attempting to catch her breath. She smiled despite her flushed feeling, removed his laptop from the nightstand, and handed it to him.

"Read your notes," she again announced.

He reluctantly accepted his laptop. She knew she needed to get away from Harlan before she talked herself into doing something she'd later regret...again. Indy hurried for the bathroom and shut the door behind her.

Chapter Thirty-one

Only a moment later, Indy appeared on the backstairs to the dimly lit kitchen. She repeatedly ran her fingers through her mussed hair while simultaneously fighting her guilt and lust. She approached the refrigerator, hoping a cold drink would help douse the fire burning within her. She suddenly shivered from how cold the kitchen felt, appeared bewildered, and looked to the partially open back door. It only took a split second for alarm to sweep through her. Indy ran for the stairs. A man, dressed head-to-toe in black, suddenly appeared before her, blocking her path to the backstairs. Indy jumped back a step with a startled scream. As he lunged for her, she spun into a roundhouse kick and struck him in the chest. He was thrown backward and roughly into the kitchen door, slamming it shut with his body. Indy attempted to run past him for the stairs. The intruder recovered too quickly and tackled her to the floor. His weight combined with the hard landing nearly knocked the wind out of her, but she managed to struggle against him as he fought to subdue her. More so than a cry for help, she needed to get out a warning to the defenseless, nearly clueless man upstairs.

"Harlan!"

There was a faint thump from upstairs followed immediately by a crash. Indy's heart leaped into her throat. Someone was already upstairs! She'd left Harlan alone and defenseless in his confused condition. Her momentary hesitation was all the man on top of her needed to subdue her. He caught both her wrists, pulled her to her feet, and body slammed her on top of the kitchen table. His hand gripped her throat, nearly suffocating her while holding her to the table. She struggled against his crushing hand while gasping to catch her breath. He was no ordinary intruder. She was almost certain he could crush her windpipe, if it had been his intention. As she struggled to loosen his grip, she thrashed with her legs in a frantic attempt to kick any part of him she could reach. Her attacker seemed to know exactly where to stand to avoid her kicks. With his free hand, he removed a hunting knife.

There was a loud thump from upstairs, indicating Harlan was in trouble. For a split second, Indy's mind commanded rational thought if she intended to save Harlan. Despite her slightly dizzy feeling from lack of air, Indy assessed her position and the intruder's. He stepped in closer in order to plunge the knife downward into her chest. It was the split second she needed to connect with his body. Indy found her connection point and kicked the man in the groin. It wasn't her best shot, but it was enough to send the man back a step and clutch himself in agony. Indy sprang up from the table and barely took a moment to catch her breath.

"Harlan, I'm coming!"

The intruder had recovered quicker than anticipated, stepped in front of her, and blocked her path while holding the knife clutched firmly in his hand. To his surprise, Indy kicked the knife from his hand, knocking it across the floor. Before he could react, she kicked him in the ribs and then in the head. As he fell against the counter, Indy followed through with two karate punches to his face. As she went for the third, he grabbed her wrist. This time she was ready for him. Indy kneed him in the ribs then spun into a high roundhouse kick, striking him in the face. He was thrown violently to the floor from the hard strike.

Before Indy could react, there was a loud thumping on the backstairs as someone tumbled down them in the darkness and collapsed to the floor at the bottom of the steps. Indy gasped with horror and ran for the motionless man. As she was just about upon him, she suddenly stopped. It was the second intruder who had fallen down the stairs! Indy was suddenly grabbed from behind by the man whom she thought had been disabled. He clutched her around the waist with one arm and had her in a chokehold around her neck with the other arm. She fought against him, but he held her in a python like grip. The intruder subdued her then glared at the second man lying on the floor.

"Come on, man, get up!"

The second intruder finally groaned and slowly moved to his feet while gingerly touching the blood on his temple. Harlan silently appeared on the backstairs in only his boxer shorts. He hadn't made a sound and his emotionless stare was cause for alarm. The second intruder saw him out of the corner of his eye, appeared alarmed, and attempted to bolt away from him. Harlan grabbed his arm and kicked him several times in the ribs with precise, fierce jabs. He released the intruder then spun into a high roundhouse kick, striking him in the face, and propelling him onto the kitchen table. The heavy table squealed as it moved several inches from the hard hit. The first intruder appeared alarmed as his partner lie motionless on the table. He looked back at Harlan while clinging to Indy. His arm tightened around her neck in a position she'd recognized as a neck breaker. Whoever they were; they were highly trained.

"Stay back or I'll snap her neck," he warned Harlan with a hint of fear in his tone.

Harlan's expression was impossible to read, and there was no telling what was going through his mind. He stood perfectly still in attack position, as if awaiting some secret signal to strike. Indy knew the situation was a setup, and neither of them were meant to survive the home invasion. It was life-or-death, and she needed to make a decision. With every ounce of strength she could manage, Indy rammed her elbow into the man's ribs. She knew it wouldn't be enough to take him down, and he'd kill her after the split second it took him to recover. In the brief second he released her, Indy leaped onto the island counter to put as much distance between her and the intruder as possible. She was accurate on his quick recovery, but that split second was all she needed.

Harlan reacted with no warning, immediately striking. He spun into another high, fast roundhouse kick, striking the first intruder in the head. He was thrown roughly against the counter, almost flying into Indy where she sat clinging to her knees to avoid the collision. He bounced off the granite and dropped to the floor. The second intruder rolled off the table with his knife clutched in his hand and attempted to slash Harlan, whose attention remained on the man hitting the floor. Although it seemed as if Harlan hadn't been paying attention, he deflected the blow and gave the intruder a sharp shot to his wrist. The knife flew out of his hand and up in the air. Harlan caught the knife mid-air, skillfully flipped it, and thrust it into the man's neck. He gurgled a gasp as blood ran from his mouth while staring Harlan in the eyes. Harlan's expression remained unchanged and without emotion or mercy.

As the second intruder sank to the floor, Harlan stared at the dead man a moment then claimed the first intruder's discarded knife. He clutched it in a fashion that sent fear through Indy. He looked at Indy, who remained on the counter while breathing heavily as she stared at the man bleeding out onto the floor. She couldn't be certain, but she believed the man at the base of the counter was dead also. Harlan's expression finally softened and a strange realization seemed to cross his face as he stared at her.

"Are you okay?" he asked softly.

Indy met his gaze and attempted to relax as she slowly slid off the counter near him. She continued to breathe heavily and had a hard time getting the words to come out. She managed a nod.

"Yeah," she gasped softly.

Harlan's entire body sagged with relief as he pulled her into his arms and held her against him. She trembled slightly in his arms. She'd never witnessed *that* side of Harlan before. Her father had been right; she didn't really know who Harlan was. The more her body trembled, the firmer he clung to her in an attempt to stop her trembling. He suddenly gasped and pulled back to meet her gaze. His eyes were wide with a look of panic in them.

"They were bad guys, right?" he suddenly asked, as if fearing the reality of what had just happened. "They tried to kill us, didn't they?"

"Yes, they were bad guys," she said softly and pulled him back against her. "You did the right thing."

It was now Harlan's turn to tremble. She heard the knife fall from his hand and clatter as it struck the tile floor.

Chapter Thirty-two

Not more than ten minutes had passed after the attack in the kitchen. Indy paced Harlan's ransacked bedroom with the cordless phone to her ear and watched Harlan change into his street clothes. He seemed to be off in another world, and his sluggish actions reinforced it. Whatever had transpired between Harlan and the intruder in his bedroom had resulted in damage to the lamp, his laptop, and the bed, which had most of the linen torn from it. Despite her conversation with Roman over the phone, she couldn't help but study Harlan's odd behavior. Something was seriously wrong in his mind, and it frightened her. She still wanted to change into something more appropriate before Roman arrived at the crime scene, which was once her kitchen. She wasn't sure she'd have enough time, and she certainly couldn't leave Harlan alone. Harlan was going to require extensive damage control to bring him back to an acceptable level of coherence. She heard Roman's voice on the other end, bringing her out of her trance.

"Yeah, I'm still here, Roman," she announced while attempting to sound strong despite everything she'd already been through tonight. She continued to watch Harlan fumbling with the buttons on his shirt.

More than her own trauma, she feared for Harlan's recovery. "We'll meet you in the foyer in ten minutes."

She again looked at Harlan. He had finally finished dressing and now held the television remote control. His finger pressed the button gaining vigor as he stared blankly across the room. Indy felt her heart pounding in her chest. She didn't have a good feeling about his state of mind and hoped the earlier incident hadn't seriously disrupted his rehabilitation. Although, if she were honest with herself, he was already acting strangely before the kitchen assault. She placed her attention back on her phone call.

"Listen, I have to go," she announced. "Harlan's acting, well, odd. I need to do *something* about it." There was an awkward pause as she listened to Roman on the other end. "Yeah, I still have what the doctor gave me. I'll use it if necessary." Indy kept her attention focused on Harlan. "Yes, ten minutes," she replied then disconnected the call. She watched Harlan as he stood by the bed and pressed the remote control button with increasing agitation. "Roman's on his way."

Harlan didn't respond. Indy slowly approached him and attempted to read the look on his face as he stared blankly at the wall. She didn't know where he was, but he was definitely gone from their world.

"Are you okay?" she asked gently.

There was no response. His finger repeatedly struck the remote control button faster and with more aggression. As she stared into his eyes, she saw them shifting back and forth as if reading from some unseen textbook.

"Harlan," she demanded his attention.

His expression suddenly dropped as if something struck him hard. Harlan turned and bolted from the room. Indy let out a terrified cry and ran after him.

"Harlan, wait! What's wrong?"

Indy chased after him along the second floor hallway. He entered her father's bedroom and stopped just a few feet inside the room. Indy entered and paused in the doorway behind him. She watched him with concern, frightened of his next outburst. Harlan's eyes shifted across the room in a state near panic.

"Please have locked the guns up," Indy muttered softly.

Harlan suddenly spun to face her with a look that frightened her. His finger pounded on the remote control button with such force, the plastic casing cracked. He'd gone mad!

"The coyote," he announced with concern. "Don't you see? It was the coyote all along!"

Before Indy had a chance to react, Harlan dropped the broken remote control, took a quick step toward her, and grabbed her arms. She jumped with surprise to his sudden movement.

"The coyote wants me dead!"

She stared into his confused eyes with fear. She needed to do something, but she wasn't sure what. Roman would be at the house in a few minutes, but she couldn't trust Harlan around her friend, not in his current condition. Before she could come up with a response or an intelligent solution, Harlan approached the tall dresser and began tearing things from the drawer. Indy watched in horror as her father's boxer shorts and socks were thrown haphazard across the room.

"What are you doing?" she gasped while subconsciously running her fingers through her hair. She finally glared at him and took a firm approach. "Stop this, Harlan!"

Harlan crossed the room to a second dresser, pulled the drawer open, and tossed pairs of pants across the floor. Aggression wasn't going to solve anything, and he wasn't interested in listening to her. She had only one card left to play. Indy hurried from the room. She returned only a moment later with a sedation syringe hidden behind her back.

"Harlan, you need to stop this," she announced in a firm but comforting tone.

He didn't respond to her words.

She drew a deep breath and spoke softer. "Please, you're scaring me."

Harlan straightened and turned to face her. Her words broke through, causing him to stare at her with concern for her feelings. His lips parted to speak, but he suddenly froze and no words came out. Harlan's look suddenly hardened and renewed hostility swept over him like a tidal wave. Harlan bolted across the room for her. Indy gasped and jumped backward, striking the nightstand behind her and clutching the sedation syringe close to her side so he wouldn't see it. Harlan reached past her and grabbed the framed picture of Liz. He stared at the picture with increasing hostility and aggression. He tossed the picture to the bed and pulled open the drawer she leaned against, nearly knocking her aside. Harlan removed a semiautomatic pistol from the drawer. Indy suddenly gasped and jumped away from him. She couldn't believe her father left a gun in the drawer with Harlan not yet himself. Certainly, her father wouldn't have left it loaded. Harlan skillfully popped the clip, checked that it contained bullets, and then slammed it back in with added vigor. Indy jumped with alarm as he swiftly cocked the gun. The sound alone was enough to send chills down her spine. She slowly moved toward him.

"Harlan," she announced gently, "put down the gun."

Harlan glared at her as if surprised by her comment. He snatched the discarded, framed picture from the bed and vigorously shook it at Indy.

"The coyote," he growled his discontent. "The coyote tried to kill me."

"Please put down the gun," Indy whispered without taking her eyes from his.

"Why aren't you listening?" he demanded, clearly frustrated, while staring back at her.

"Put down the gun and I'll listen," she replied gently.

Harlan stared at her a moment, groaned softly, and set the gun on the nightstand between them. Indy moved closer to him where he stood just before the bed. She gently touched his face with her left hand and stared into his eyes.

"Okay, now what are you talking about?"

Harlan inhaled deeply and placed his hand on hers that touched his cheek. He shut his eyes and sighed softly to the feel of her hand. Indy took a step closer to him while keeping him focused on her hand touching his face. She gently slipped her right arm around his waist. Her right hand concealed the syringe, which she carefully positioned over his buttocks. Before she could even coil back with the syringe behind him, Harlan grabbed her wrist and snatched the injection from her. His instincts and reflexes were enough to stun her. Harlan held the syringe and stared at her with a look of surprise and possible hostility.

"Bad girl," he growled softly.

Before she had a chance to speak in her defense, Harlan injected the needle into her buttocks. Indy let out a startled gasp to the sharp sting. Harlan removed the needle, casually set it aside, and pushed her onto the bed. She bounced slightly in a sitting position. Harlan reclaimed the gun from the nightstand. Indy attempted to protest but she suddenly felt her head spinning. She was unable to focus on him. She clutched her head and attempted to remain alert. Harlan placed the gun down the back of his pants and removed an extra clip from the drawer. He turned to Indy. She made an attempt to stand. Harlan placed a hand on her shoulder and easily returned her to the bed. She stared helplessly at him and knew she was going to be unconscious any second. Harlan stared into her eyes as she attempted to focus on him. He gently lowered her to a relaxed position on the bed and leaned over her. A devious smile crossed his face as he stared into her eyes from only a few inches from her face.

"After I kill the coyote, it's my turn to interrogate you," he whispered in a seductive tone.

Harlan kissed her quickly but passionately on the mouth then straightened and left the room. Indy lie on the bed and stared after him as the room spun. Everything became dark.

Chapter Thirty-three

Indy slowly woke while lying on the bed to Roman hovering over her while speaking. She could hear his words, but it sounded as if he was talking in a foreign language. She wasn't sure where she was or what had happened. She slowly looked around the room with disorientation. It took her only a moment to realize that she was in her father's room, but she couldn't remember how she got there or what had happened prior to that. Roman appeared relieved that she was finally awake, clung to her hand, and groaned softly as he sat facing her on the bed.

"Oh, thank God," he announced. "After I saw the dead men in the kitchen, I thought you were dead too." His look suddenly turned stern. "You told me some men broke into your house. Why didn't you tell me they were dead?"

Indy slowly sat up while clutching her head and immediately groaned from the tremendous pounding she felt. Roman attempted to steady her as she sat hunched over.

"Whoa, take it easy," he remarked while studying her. "Want to tell me what happened?"

Indy's mind raced as she attempted to piece together what had happened leading up until the time she woke to Roman over her bedside. Then it came back to her. Alarm swept over her, and she looked at Roman.

"Where's Harlan?"

"I didn't see him," he replied and appeared curious. "Indy, what happened?"

"After we were attacked, Harlan was acting really strange," she informed him. "He thought Liz was the evil coyote. I tried to stop him, but he grabbed the sedation syringe and used it on me instead." She stared at her friend with concern. "We have to find him, Roman."

Indy attempted to get out of bed, despite her slightly spinning head. Roman helped steady her on her feet.

"We should search the house. Maybe he never left," Roman remarked. "You know his mind."

"Yes, I know his mind, and he's not in his right one," she insisted. Her look turned grave. "He found my father's gun. We need to find him."

"He's armed?" Roman suddenly gasped then stared at her with renewed concern. He seemed ill prepared for what might happen next. "That's not good. I really think we need to call Sheriff Lerner in on this."

"If we find him, I can talk him down," she insisted. "I don't think he'd actually hurt Liz."

Roman didn't seem to share her conviction. "Did he kill those men downstairs?"

She stared at him with surprise and almost feared answering the question. "That's different," Indy informed him. "That was self-defense."

"What if he thinks killing Liz is self-defense?"

Indy couldn't fight the horrible feeling burning inside her. She didn't want to believe it, and no matter what she thought, she was never going to admit it aloud.

"Can we do this later?"

Roman stared at her with a look that caused her concern. It was as if he were harboring some dark secret. She felt the need to stare at him and wait for whatever it was he had to say.

"There's something I need to tell you, Indy, and you're not going to like it," Roman gently announced. He took a deep, nervous breath as she stared at him with anticipation. "On Christmas night, I'd gone into the kitchen to make Harlan some tea. I swear I'd only left him alone for five minutes. When I returned to his room, that woman was lying dead on the floor."

Indy felt her entire body tense at the words she was hearing for the first time. Roman wouldn't lie about something like that, but she just couldn't believe it was true.

"Harlan broke her neck," he announced firmly, driving the pain a little deeper into her heart. "I'd only found out later who she was."

It then occurred to Indy, she wasn't the only one who couldn't accept what Harlan had done. It would have been impossible for Harlan to move the dead nurse's body.

"What did you do?" she gasped with surprise, although she already knew the answer.

"I didn't know what to do," Roman continued while nearly trembling from his own words. "I panicked. I didn't know why she came back, but there had to be some reason why he did it." Roman stared into Indy's panic-filled eyes and inhaled deeply. "I carried her out to the main road and dumped her in the swamp. He subconsciously ran his fingers violently through his hair and could barely look at her. "It was wrong, I know, but I knew Harlan didn't kill her without reason. I couldn't let them put him away when he couldn't tell his side."

"Is that why his cast was all scratched out?"

"Yeah," he replied with a deep sigh. "When I came back from dumping the body, he had already written it on his cast. I had to remove the evidence, so I crossed out a whole bunch of things to make it look random."

"And now you're having second thoughts?"

"She obviously slipped in through the terrace door in his bedroom, but did that justify him killing her?" Roman remarked while staring at her. He tilted his head with concern. "I don't know what to think. He's trained to kill and, at the moment, he's somewhat delusional. I'm not sure he's capable of rational thinking. Are you willing to gamble with Liz's life?"

"I know you have to do your job, Roman, but can't we leave Sheriff Lerner out of this for now?" Indy pleaded while searching his eyes. "Call Liz at the funeral home. You can keep her safe until I find Harlan."

"It's five in the morning," Roman informed her. "I'm sure they're both still sleeping. They have a big funeral in the morning. I doubt anyone will answer."

"Then we'll go to the funeral home," Indy insisted. "Harlan may be a genius, but he doesn't even know her name. He certainly wouldn't know to look for her at the funeral home."

"Okay, we'll go to the funeral home," Roman reluctantly agreed. "I'll stay with Liz for a few hours, but if you don't find Harlan in that time, I have to report it to Sheriff Lerner."

Indy nodded and sighed softly. "Fine."

†

Roman's police cruiser pulled up the long driveway to the out-of-the-way funeral home on the hill. Liz's car was parked around the side of the funeral home not far from the hearse. Kale's car wasn't in front, which was unusual. The funeral home appeared quiet, although that was typical for the early hour. Indy and Roman got out of his police cruiser and approached the front door. It seemed odd that the interior lights were on. Roman knocked, but there was no answer. Indy tried the door. It was unlocked! They exchanged looks. Roman entered with Indy bringing up the rear. Both looked around the quiet foyer and grand hallway. Was it possible they were already up and preparing for the large, morning funeral?

"Kale?" Indy called out while looking around where she stood in the large hallway.

There was no response.

"Maybe he's in the embalming room downstairs," Roman suggested.

"Perhaps," she announced, although she was certain the body would already be upstairs in one of the viewing rooms for the morning funeral.

As they walked along the hallway, Indy peered into the front viewing room to the right. The lavish room was prepared for a massive funeral and filled with flowers. The casket set stately toward the back of the room with the lid closed. Why was the lid closed? Indy suddenly hesitated and quickly entered the viewing room. Roman was surprised by her change of direction and hurried after her. Indy crossed the room in a hurry then slowed her approach to see several droplets of blood along the floor. As she got closer to the closed casket, she saw a faint, bloody handprint on the casket lid. Indy stopped a couple of feet from the casket and cast a horrified look at Roman. Both lunged for the casket. Roman hesitated then uncertainly opened the lid.

Both stared with horror at Margo lying motionless within the casket. A small amount of bright red blood glared at them as it stained the white, satin pillow beneath her head. Indy cried out with surprise and horror. Her first instinct was to see if her friend was alive or dead, but she feared finding out. Before she could convince her body to move closer to her motionless, bleeding friend, they heard movement behind them. Both turned to the sound. Indy felt a surge of pain against her head but barely saw the blur that had struck her. She collapsed to the floor without a chance to brace her sudden fall. Indy attempted to keep her eyes open despite everything turning fuzzy and dark. The only sound she heard was a loud humming coming from the confines of her own mind.

She could see the blurred image of Roman struggling with someone not far from her. She wanted to help, but she couldn't even convince her fingers to move. Roman punched the man in the face, and for a moment, Indy felt relief that her friend had gotten the upper hand in their attack. She clutched and clawed at the floor, hoping she was closer to pulling herself up, when, in fact, she'd done little more than move her fingers across the hardwood floor. The distinctive crack of a gunshot was suddenly heard above the loud humming sound in her head. Indy then saw the blurred image of Roman being thrown backward and against the casket. He collapsed to the floor near her. She could barely make out his face and his uniform, but she could see the blood seeping from his body onto the hardwood floor not far from her. Indy attempted to reach for him, but her fingers barely moved. She stared at his motionless face before everything went dark.

Chapter Thirty-four

Indy slowly woke to complete darkness and a feeling of dizzying disorientation. She had no idea where she was, since it was so dark. Her head was still spinning and thumping with tremendous pain as if she'd been--? Horror swept over her along with the shocking realization of what had happened back at the funeral home. She immediately thrust her palms upward, connecting with a firm surface covered in a satin lining. As she felt around the small, enclosed area, panic overtook her. She was locked inside a casket! Indy pounded the inside lid with her palms while screaming hysterically.

On the outside, the casket was secured on a retractable gurney, which was elevated only a few feet from the floor of the oddly bland looking room. The room was filled with several crates of varying sizes and a loud humming sound was almost deafening. Despite the loud humming, thumping was heard from within the vibrating casket along with Indy's muffled screams. Unfortunately, there was no one around to hear her faint cries or witness the vibrating death container. The casket became still and all sounds within it subsided. A loud bang suddenly rocked the casket. A second bang immediately followed. The casket toppled over and struck the floor with a tremendous crash, breaking the lid seal. With the third bang, the casket lid flew open. Indy rolled out of the casket and sprang to her feet in attack position. Despite her dizziness and the blood streaking the side of her face from her temple laceration, she was prepared for a fight. She looked around the crate filled holding room and listened to the familiar humming sound. Her expression suddenly dropped with the knowledge of where she was. She was in the cargo hold of a plane!

Realizing she was alone within the cargo hold, she relaxed her defensive position, tenderly touched her bloodied head, and looked around to assess her situation, which obviously wasn't good. How could she be in the cargo hold of a plane? How was that even possible? Who had her? Where were they taking her? Her gaze fell upon two other caskets within the enclosure. One of the caskets had the familiar, bloody handprint on the lid.

"Margo," Indy gasped softly.

She looked around the cargo hold interior, saw some discarded tools, and grabbed a crowbar. She returned to the casket and, with much effort, pried the lid open. As she opened the lid, Indy's expression dropped at the sight of Margo's motionless body. Margo suddenly cried out and sprayed something in Indy's face. Indy jumped back with a startled scream and touched the liquid on her face as Margo sat up. Margo stared at Indy with alarm and gasped, placing her hand to her mouth. Indy wiped the liquid from her face with bewilderment and looked at Margo.

"What the hell is that?"

"Breath freshener," Margo replied while attempting to relax from her harrowing ordeal. "Sorry, I thought you were the bastard who nabbed me."

Indy helped Margo from the casket. Her friend nearly collapsed to the floor and clutched her own bleeding head. She knew how her friend felt.

"Who nabbed you?" Indy asked while keeping her friend from falling.

Margo slowly shook her head while glancing around then looked back at Indy. "I didn't see him. He got me inside my car as I was leaving your house," she announced and again looked around. "Where the hell are we?"

"Your guess is as good as mine."

Margo continued to look around and appeared bewildered. She looked back at Indy with surprise. "Are we in a plane?" she suddenly gasped.

"Unfortunately, yes. I don't know how long I was out," Indy informed her and leaned against the casket. "Which means we could be anywhere."

"I was tied up in some sort of basement for what seemed like hours after they nabbed me," Margo said while frowning her annoyance. "Whoever took me kept me sedated and blindfolded. I could feel them sticking me with a needle."

"Roman and I didn't find you until morning," Indy informed her. "You were in that basement nearly eight hours."

Margo glanced at her watch. "It's one o'clock," she announced while insecurely rubbing her wrist.

"So that means it's been eight hours since we first found you at the funeral home," Indy remarked. "That's not good. We *literally* could be anywhere in the world right now."

Margo stared at Indy and appeared tense by her own realization. "You said you and Roman found me," she announced with concern. "Where's Roman?"

Indy frowned, ran her fingers through her hair partly matted with dried blood, and slowly looked down. Although the details were fuzzy, she knew the outcome.

"They shot him," Indy replied softly then finally met Margo's gaze while fighting her tears. "I don't think he made it. Even if he survived, I doubt they would have let him live."

Margo stared at Indy with horror and possible disbelief. Her look hardened into something hateful. "We need to be ready for these bastards."

"They have a private plane, which means they have money," Indy informed her while frantically searching for the best explanation to their situation. "If they have money, that means they have some pretty serious firepower."

"If they shot a police officer, we're expendable too," Margo remarked in a stern tone as her anger continued to rise. "Remember who your father is, Indy. If we're going to survive, you need to become him and fast."

They heard pounding and screaming from the third casket, startling them. Both women lunged for the casket. Indy pried the lid open with the crowbar while Margo pulled on the lid in an attempt to help. The lid flew open to reveal the frightened and slightly battered Liz. Her hair was also matted with blood, obviously having been knocked out as well. She looked at both women while gasping.

"What happened?" Liz suddenly asked.

"Liz?" Indy gasped while attempting to make sense of their situation. She stared at her father's girlfriend a moment then a horrible realization suddenly hit her and her expression dropped. "I think I know why they kept us alive, and I think I know where they're taking us."

"You do?" Margo cried out. "Where?"

"Santiago's compound."

"Santiago? Who's Santiago?" Margo demanded.

Liz appeared horrified while staring at them with disbelief then struggled to get out of the casket. "That corrupt nationalist Flynn captured?"

Indy and Margo helped Liz out of the casket and to her feet. She seemed slightly unstable and clutched her head. Her concern for her own welfare quickly dissipated.

"But he's incarcerated," Liz informed them. "Flynn said they had him at some secret holding facility."

"And his men intend to use us to get him back," Indy announced while frowning.

"Flynn will save us, I know he will," Liz informed them while wrenching her fingers together. "It's what he does. That's what he does, right?" She no longer sounded convinced.

"He'll try, but these aren't the sort of people who keep their promises," Indy remarked while feeling the pressure of the situation. "My father knows that."

There was an awkward silence among the three. It wasn't the reassurance either wanted to hear.

"What do we do?" Margo finally asked.

Indy inhaled deeply and stared at both women. "We need a really good plan."

Margo stared at Indy's expression and appeared concerned. "There's something else, isn't there?" she suddenly asked. "What aren't you telling us?"

Indy ignored the question and began a frantic search of the cargo hold for any other weapon besides the crowbar. She approached the open toolbox and routed through it. Margo and Liz quickly joined her, the strain of concern clearly on their faces. Indy hesitated while staring into the toolbox. She picked up a utility knife, staring at it only a moment, and then removed a roll of electrical tape.

"Indy," Margo announced with concern in her voice. "What aren't you telling us? We have a right to know."

Indy inhaled deeply and glanced back at her friend. She didn't know what to say to her. Margo stared at the look on Indy's face. Her expression shattered.

"They're going to kill me first, aren't they?" Margo suddenly gasped.

Indy didn't respond and returned her attention to the toolbox before her. Margo stared a moment longer in silence and seemed to come to her own conclusion.

"That's why they nabbed me," Margo cried out, still unable to move. "They're going to kill me to show your father how serious they are."

Liz stared at both women with the same look of horror. Her expression matched Margo's terrified look. "Then I'm next."

Indy spun to face them with a stern, determined look. "That won't happen. We're going to stop it," she announced, although she was having a tough time convincing herself of that. "We have a crowbar we can use to defend ourselves, but we need to find some better weapons."

"You're telling us they have automatic weapons, and you intend to fight them with a crowbar?" Margo suddenly demanded. "We'll be ripped to shreds!"

Indy spun to face Margo with a stern and determined look on her face.

"We don't have a lot of options," Indy boldly informed her. "Running, hiding, and fighting. That's it."

"Well," Margo announced with a sigh, "there's certainly no place to run."

"Can't exactly hide either," Liz muttered.

"Exactly," Indy replied. "So we have no choice. We have to fight."

"Do you have a plan?" Margo asked, appearing fearful while rubbing her chilled arms.

Indy reluctantly nodded. "Yeah, I have a plan," she replied. "But you're not going to like it."

†

The large, private plane landed on the moderately overgrown airstrip at the abandoned airfield. Once the plane was at a complete stop, ten heavily armed men gathered around the cargo ramp and watched it lower. They had their assault rifles leveled and prepared to fire. The cargo area was quiet and void of life. All ten men stormed into the cargo hold and remained at the ready. Two men approached the three closed caskets, now returned to their upright position, and opened each. All three were empty. One of the men indicated for the others to scatter and search the cargo hold. Indy silently dropped down behind them into a crouched position with a metal pole clutched in her hands. As they turned, she straightened and fiercely struck them with the pole, displaying amazing skill and precision with each hit. She successfully disarmed four men before a fifth grabbed her from behind. Indy rammed her elbow into his ribs and flipped him over her shoulder. She struck two more men before several surrounded her with their assault rifles aimed. Indy clung to her pole and stared at the armed men. It had been a brave battle, even if she knew she had no chance of winning. She frowned and dropped her pole in surrender.

"Find the other two," the undisputed leader ordered the remaining guards.

As the men scattered to search the cargo hold, two armed men pushed Margo and Liz up the ramp and back into the plane. Both women eyed Indy with looks of shame, having been caught and ruining the plan.

"We found these two fleeing the scene," one of the guards announced.

The leader eyed the two women then looked back at Indy and grinned in an almost approving manner.

"Nice diversion," he announced and held back his chuckle. "You've already figured out we can't risk killing you, so you thought you'd arrange for your friends' escape. That was rather smart...and a little dumb."

He then nodded to the guard standing alongside Margo. The guard punched Margo in the face, knocking her to the metal, cargo floor. She clutched her cheek and writhed in agony. Indy's body twitched in reaction as she stared at her injured friend. She refrained from screaming like a hysterical woman, although she wanted to run to Margo's side and comfort her. It was, after all, her fault her friend was involved.

The leader stared into Indy's eyes and grinned slyly. "Try that again, and your friends will suffer greatly. Do we understand one another?"

Indy cast a look at Margo as she slowly moved to her knees while clutching her reddened cheek. Indy looked back at the man standing before her, frowned, and nodded. She understood his position and disregard for Margo and Liz's lives. It was a calculated risk to save her friends, especially since she knew she was worth more to them alive at the moment. They were counting on her father doing anything in his power to save his daughter, including sacrificing himself. They thought they were so smart. What they didn't count on was Indy's willingness to sacrifice her own life for her father's...and that would be their downfall.

Chapter Thirty-five

What remained of Santiago's intact compound was little more than part of the mansion, resembling a medieval castle after surviving a lengthy battle. The entire jungle setting surrounding the standing structure and piles of rubble was peaceful in the evening setting. Several American soldiers patrolled the exterior of what remained of the intact building. There were several lights on within the building and a few temporary generators kept the exterior well-lit for the soldiers standing guard. The brief sound of parting air was barely heard. One of the soldiers gasped, clutched his bleeding neck, and fell to the ground. As another soldier ran to aid him, he was silently struck down as well.

Flynn and Jackson were within the massive dining room, sitting at the lavish, carved table with enough seating for a gathering of twenty. The table was loaded with scorched document boxes and stacks of singed papers. Each man sifted through boxes filled with equally charred papers. Some crumbled in their hands, leaving both men disgusted and frustrated with their current assignment. Flynn stretched his back with a groan.

"All things being equal, I'd rather be storming the trenches than sifting through this crap," Flynn remarked.

Jackson allowed his temple to fall against his fist while holding up his head. "We only have one hundred and six boxes to go," he muttered.

Flynn groaned, placed his hands behind his neck, and stared up at the mural painted on the cathedral ceiling high above them. "I wish Harlan were here."

"Why would you want to punish him?" Jackson asked while lifting his head and looking at his commander. "He'd be more miserable than you." He looked back at the stack of papers in front of him. He then muttered, "You're bad enough."

"Yeah, but then he'd blow the place up and we could all go home," Flynn announced as he leaned forward over his mound of charred papers. He sank into thought and appeared distant. "Maybe I should call Indy and make sure everything is okay."

"You left two messages," Jackson replied without looking at him. "She'll call you back."

Flynn groaned and stared at the papers without touching them. "I shouldn't have left them."

"They're fine, Flynn."

"I know, it's just--" he again leaned back and sighed softly. "I'm tired of leaving my little girl. My entire life has been a series of 'hello' and 'goodbyes'. Maybe I'm just getting old."

Jackson looked at Flynn and appeared curious. "Are you thinking about retiring?"

"Maybe," he replied with a sigh then frowned. "No. I couldn't do that to you and Nate. If you got killed on some botched mission, I'd never forgive myself."

Jackson sat up straight in his chair and stared his commander in the eyes. "You're forgetting something, Flynn."

"What's that?"

"You go, we go," Jackson replied. "Nate and I would never survive another commander. We barely survived you." He casually shrugged. "Besides, if Harlan can't return to active duty, it just won't be the same."

Flynn sank into thought and reluctantly nodded. "I've been thinking about that a lot too."

Nate hurried into the room with his assault rifle cradled in his arms like a cherished baby. He appeared out of breath and moderately annoyed.

"Security isn't answering," Nate announced gruffly.

Both men seated at the table became alert and straightened while staring at the intimidating man.

"Which ones?" Flynn demanded.

"All of them."

Both men jumped up from their seats and grabbed their nearby assault rifles. They cocked the rifles with added vigor.

Flynn's expression turned stern. "Let's treat this as a situation, boys," he announced.

All three armed men hurried from the room.

†

Indy was tied to an elegant, wooden chair in the stunning, massive wine cellar. Despite having been tied and blindfolded for her arrival, she was almost certain they had brought her to the compound her father and his team had seized on their last mission. Or, in Harlan's case, the compound he blew up. She could still smell the charred remains, and the surrounding area had that humid, vegetation smell, indicating a jungle setting. If she was at Santiago's compound, there was the distinct possibility her father, Jackson, and Nate were close to where they were holding her captive. The thought of her father and his remaining team being close by was both comforting and terrifying. She looked around the wine cellar to familiarize herself with her surroundings. If she hadn't been concerned for her situation and the welfare of those she loved, she'd be impressed by the massive wine cellar. It was made of stone, like some medieval dungeon. There were huge, wooden kegs as well as thousands of bottles of wine stacked neatly in tiny slots.

The wine cellar's layout was important, since she knew there would be only one way in and out with a very thick, heavy door. A rescue would come with a steep price to anyone attempting to save her. The wine cellar's only saving grace was ample places to dodge flying bullets. She knew her situation was bad, but she couldn't stop thinking about Margo and Liz. They would be the ones who would suffer first as means to get her father's attention. If a rescue did come for her, she worried for the safety of her father and the team she loved dearly. That left only one option in Indy's mind. She'd need to save herself and give the others a fighting chance. Indy glared at the two, armed guards, Hugo and Miles, who stood before her. She couldn't deny, by the pang in her stomach and the pounding of her heart, that she was frightened, but the thought of the others dying allowed her anger to take control. She'd spent enough time in the company of some of the military's finest bad asses that some of it was bound to rub off on her. Her look hardened and her eyes narrowed as the Stryker in her surfaced.

"Where are my friends?" she demanded.

"They're safe--for now, but if you attempt to escape, we will see that they suffer before we kill them," Hugo, the obvious, self-proclaimed leader of the two, informed her. "We need you alive. We don't need them at all." His smirk mocked her. "Remember that."

She would be sure to remember that. She would also remember to kill him first, if given the opportunity. Indy hadn't realized she was staring at him until his eyes narrowed while staring back at her. It wasn't that he feared her, but she could tell he didn't like the way she stared at him without cowering. Hugo left the wine cellar without another word. Miles removed a bottle of wine from the nearby rack, looked at the label, grinned his approval, and opened it with his teeth. Indy cast her attention upon the brawny man and watched him closely. He was the 'Nate' of Santiago's group. She wondered if the all-brawn man shared Nate's special brand of intellect as well. Nate wasn't easily fooled, but he could be talked in circles. The intercom crackled, startling her.

"Good evening, Commander Flynn," Hugo's voice announced over the intercom. "As you are aware, you have something we want. Well, now we have something you want."

Miles moved behind Indy, placed a semiautomatic to her temple, and grinned while indicating the camera on the table directly in front of her.

"Smile for the camera, sweetheart," Miles announced.

†

Nate hurried into the massive, two-story library through the glass patio doors and joined Jackson and Flynn, who stared at a television screen mounted on the wall near the tall rows of bookcases. A close-up image revealed Indy tied to the chair with the gun to her temple. The scenery behind her was successfully blocked, preventing them from seeing where she was being held. Flynn stared at his daughter with a gun to her head and sneered with silent rage. Jackson just stared with his mouth hanging open.

"Oh, shit," Jackson gasped.

"But wait, there's more," Hugo's voice announced over the intercom.

The image switched to similar scenes with Margo and Liz. Both were tied in locations unknown while men held guns to their heads as well.

"Now that I have you attention, I'd like to initiate an exchange," Hugo announced. "You give us Santiago, and we return these lovely, young ladies with all their body parts intact." There was an effective pause, indicating Hugo was pleased with himself. "You have two hours to liberate him from that warship posing as a freighter sitting off the coast. If he's not delivered to us in two hours, we'll slit this lovely creature's throat."

All three stared at Margo on the screen. Margo's assailant pulled her head back by her hair and placed a large, military knife against her throat. Margo was seen gasping even though there was no volume to their video feed from her location.

"Then, in another two hours, we move on to the next lovely young lady," Hugo announced. "If you still don't return our captive leader, we'll move on to your attractive, young daughter." Hugo was heard chuckling softly. "But don't fear, Commander Flynn, we won't kill her right away. We'll slowly torture her hourly until you turn over Santiago." There was another pause. "As a friendly reminder, if you or your men attempt to rescue any of these women, we'll kill one to make our point. You have two hours." Hugo was heard chuckling. "Let the games begin."

The television screen went blank. Flynn stared at the screen with a look of mayhem on his hardened face. Jackson and Nate stared at Flynn with a concern neither usually displayed. This wasn't just some mission; it was personal.

"What do we do, Flynn?" Nate finally asked.

Flynn didn't even bother looking at his men. His eyes remained glued on the blank television screen. "Nate, take the jeep to the coast and contact the ship," he announced in a firm, low tone. "Don't tell them their demands."

"Then what?"

Flynn turned to face Nate and raised his brows. "You're going to bust Santiago out of the brig."

Nate appeared at a loss for words but refrained from groaning. "That won't be easy."

"You have less than two hours. Do it."

Nate uncertainly nodded and hurried from the library. Flynn spun to face Jackson with a nearly chilling look.

"You're doing some recon, Jackson," Flynn boldly announced. "I want you to locate my daughter, Margo, and Liz."

"But he said--"

"You find them and report their location," Flynn ordered. "If Nate isn't back in two hours with Santiago, we'll need to initiate a rescue."

"There are only two of us and three hostages being held in separate locations," Jackson reminded and appeared concerned. "Who do we sacrifice?"

Flynn's expression turned cold. "My daughter."

Jackson appeared horrified. "Flynn--?"

"I trained her well," Flynn launched back. "She knows the score. If they intend to kill Margo, you can bet she's already working on her own rescue. She's also the last one they'll kill." Flynn straightened proudly and stared at his friend. "We'll have more time to bargain for her life if she fails at her own rescue."

Chapter Thirty-six

One hour had passed since the demands were made for the women's safe release. Flynn paced the library while subconsciously fiddling with his semiautomatic. His mind was obviously on some plan to save the women, including his daughter, but the strain was starting to show. Jackson silently slipped in through the main door. Flynn spun with his gun aimed, prepared to shoot, saw it was just Jackson, and relaxed his grip on the trigger while lowering the gun. Despite Flynn's hostile reaction, Jackson never flinched. He was apparently used to having his comrades aim guns at him as a standard greeting.

"They're holding Liz in the lounge closest to the remains of the west wing," Jackson informed him without awaiting a demand for an update. "Margo is being held in the gatehouse." He drew a deep, concerned breath. "I couldn't find Indy. Each of the locations has a guard inside with them and one posted outside. We're looking at ten guards patrolling the estate grounds, and I'm guessing another ten inside as well."

Flynn glanced at his watch and then the clock on the wall. "We'll give Nate another thirty minutes to give us a progress report before taking our rescue positions."

"I could go back out and look for Indy," Jackson offered while fidgeting. "If I can find her--"

Flynn glared at Jackson. "No, you'll wait here until it's time. Each time you sneak around outside, we're risking the life of a hostage." He drew a deep breath and attempted to relax. "Indy will be fine. We can't worry about her, or it's going to distract from our mission to free the others. Am I clear?"

Jackson frowned and nodded. "Yes, Sir."

†

Indy remained tied to the chair in the wine cellar while watching Miles drink the expensive wine directly from the bottle in an unrefined manner. He allowed large portions of the white wine to run down his chin and onto his shirt. She couldn't imagine any man under her father's command ever behaving in such a barbaric manner. She obviously wasn't going to be able to appeal to his human side, since he didn't seem to have one. She mentally searched for another approach to engage the despicable man. Indy watched him closely, although he didn't seem to care that she stared and never bothered to look back at her.

"Are you afraid of dying?" she questioned the man while showing little emotion.

Miles glanced at her and appeared humored by the irony of the question. "You're closer to it than I am."

Indy maintained her composure and kept from flinching, even though her body wanted to react in a 'damsel in distress' sort of way. "Not from where I'm sitting."

Miles stared at her with bewilderment. She'd successfully piqued his curiosity. He smirked as he casually approached her and leaned closer to eye level with her.

"Where you're sitting, it's probably not a wise idea to piss me off," he announced in an almost mocking tone. He suddenly grinned, sending a chill down her spine. "I'm not allowed to kill you, but that leaves a whole lot of wiggle room."

Indy pushed her fears aside and mustered every ounce of strength she could to confront the large man. "Oh?" she asked while cleverly raising her brows. "Exactly what sort of wiggling did you have in mind?"

Miles stared at her a moment, as if surprised by her somewhat come-hither comment, and then grinned lustfully. "You're just begging for it, aren't you?"

"You've misjudged me," Indy announced with a slight hiss to her tone. Her eyes suddenly narrowed as she moved her face slightly closer to his face. A twisted smile crossed her lips. "I'll send you crying home to your mommy."

Miles appeared surprised by her comment and possibly the tone then laughed. Without warning, he grabbed her by the back on the neck and kissed her roughly on the mouth. Indy returned the aggressive kiss, which instinctively brought him a step closer to her as he reached for her breast. Indy suddenly kicked him in the groin, causing him to stumble backward while clutching himself with surprise and in moderate agony. Despite that he didn't go down, that split second was all Indy needed. She tossed her ropes aside along with the utility knife blade still attached to the electrical tape and leaped to her feet. Miles realized she was free from her ropes and reached for his holstered weapon. Indy spun into a high, roundhouse kick and struck him in the face. He was thrown to the floor and seemed momentarily stunned or rendered unconscious. She grabbed the discarded gun and aimed it at the motionless man.

Indy heard the click of the wine cellar door being unlocked. She spun around with the gun aimed as the door opened. A man in black combat fatigues rolled through the doorway and aimed a gun at her from his crouched position on the floor. Indy tightened her finger on the trigger then saw the familiar face. It was Harlan! She gasped with surprise and lowered her gun.

"Harlan?"

Harlan straightened while assessing the surrounding area then appeared relieved while lowering his gun as he approached her.

"Are you okay?" he asked gently.

Indy groaned with relief, threw her arms around his neck, and clung to him. "I'm so glad to see you!" She pulled away and stared at him with surprise. "How did you get here?"

"I commandeered a plane."

"You stole a plane?"

"No, I *commandeered* a plane," he reaffirmed his actions. "Big difference. When I found Roman at the funeral home--"

"Roman's alive?" she suddenly gasped.

"A little tenderized, but he's going to be fine," Harlan replied. "When Roman told me what happened, I knew who had you and why."

"You did? But how--?" It then dawned on her. She tensed slightly. "You got your memory back."

Harlan appeared slightly tense by her comment and looked away with possible embarrassment. "I'm going to need time to work on my apology, but that'll have to wait." He looked back at her, straightened proudly, and resumed combat mode. "We have twenty minutes to save Margo, but I'll need your help."

Miles attempted to stand from his position behind Indy. Before Indy even realized the man had woken, Harlan threw his knife at the man and struck him in the throat. Miles collapsed to the floor as blood seeped from his neck wound. Harlan walked past Indy, casually removed his knife from the dead man's neck, and wiped the blood on Miles' shirt. Harlan straightened and turned to face Indy. She stared at the dead man with surprise then looked back at Harlan, almost unable to speak.

"Do you have a plan?" Indy questioned as her voice crackled slightly.

"Oh, I have a plan," Harlan replied, "but it's going to require some explosives."

Indy's expression dropped.

Chapter Thirty-seven

Flynn paced the library while flexing his hand on the grip of his semiautomatic. His expression conveyed nearly every emotion possible. He had the look of an emotionally unstable man, who was contemplating ways of slowly torturing a man to death. Jackson watched his commander with silent concern. They'd never been in this sort of position before. It was never personal, and that made it frightening. They were coming down to the kidnapper's final deadline, and it would soon be time to act, setting forth a plan that would likely end unhappily for someone. Flynn looked at his watch, held his breath, and then nodded Jackson toward the terrace doors. Both men grabbed their assault rifles with purpose and headed for the glass doors.

The television suddenly came to life, interrupting their departure. Both stopped and stared at the screen. Had Nate been captured? Did something change the dynamics of their rescue attempt or even the prisoner exchange? Had Indy gotten herself killed in an attempt to rescue herself? The agony of awaiting an answer didn't last very long. The image on the screen was that of an unidentified, hooded man, tied and dangling by a rope wrapped securely around his body. Beyond the ropes binding the man, it was obvious he was dressed in the standard, orange prisoner jumpsuit used by the covert ship anchored in the ocean. There was only one person it could be beyond the black hood. Santiago!

"Greetings," came Harlan's familiar voice.

Jackson and Flynn's expressions dropped to the sound of their comrade's voice. His was the last voice they'd expected to hear at the compound. They briefly exchanged stunned looks then returned their attention back to the monitor on the wall.

"If I may direct your attention to the nearest television monitor, I'd like to introduce your long anticipated comrade," Harlan announced in a calm, confident tone. "Sorry he was a little late to the party, but he was being fitted for the latest fashion in vest bombs."

The camera zoomed in for a close-up of the vest bomb with a counter counting down from twenty minutes. The camera widened its angle to reveal the man dangling from the watchtower at the far end of the remaining compound.

"I've played your game by your rules. Here's your man," Harlan announced over the monitor. "Now we're playing my game by my rules. In less than twenty minutes, the bomb goes boom." The hint of humor could be heard in Harlan's voice. "The vest bomb is also rigged with a wireless remote. If anyone attempts to reach him, the bomb goes boom. If any of the captive women are harmed, the bomb goes...well, you know how this works." There was a moment of effective silence. "You have less than twenty minutes to release the captive woman, Margo. If she's released unharmed, the bomb counter stops. The remote will then be handed over in exchange for the remaining two hostages. You have eighteen minutes to abide by my terms. Good day."

The television screen went dead. Flynn and Jackson stared at the blank screen only a moment then exchanged looks.

"That son-of-a-bitch! He has Indy," Flynn exclaimed, expressing relief for the first time. A nervous chuckle escaped his throat as he subconsciously rubbed his bald head.

"Are you sure?"

"Trust me, he would have asked for Indy's release first," Flynn announced with renewed enthusiasm. "You go after Margo. I'm going for Liz."

Jackson nodded while sharing Flynn's confidence in their rescue operation. Both men hurried from the library with their assault rifles in hand.

†

Jackson ran alongside the stone wall near the gatehouse door while remaining low to the ground and nearly invisible in the dim lighting. He stopped not far from the gatehouse door and touched the device in his ear.

"I'm in place," he announced softly.

"So am I," Flynn responded through Jackson's earpiece. "On three. One...two...three!"

Jackson was about to leap out when the gatehouse door opened. He stopped and remained hidden. A guard appeared first. Another guard followed him with Margo, whose hands were tied before her. Jackson slung his assault rifle over his shoulder and silently leaped out from the bushes behind the man holding Margo. Before either man heard a sound, Jackson lunged for the man alongside Margo and stabbed him in the neck. Margo jumped with surprise. As the guard in front turned, Jackson knocked Margo to the ground. She fell alongside the dead man with the knife sticking out of his bleeding neck. Margo stared at the knife in the man's throat with a look of horror clearly across her face. Jackson kicked the remaining guard in the chest. He was thrown back several steps, dropping his assault rifle. The guard leaped for Jackson and tackled him harshly into the nearby wall. Jackson appeared momentarily stunned from the impact against the stone. The guard grabbed Jackson around the neck from behind and attempted to break his neck. Jackson rammed his elbow repeatedly into the guard's ribs to loosen his grip.

The guard released him and removed his semiautomatic from his holster. Jackson turned, saw the gun aimed at him, and appeared alarmed. The sound of rapid gunfire from an assault rifle broke the silence. Bullets struck the ground near them. Both turned to see Margo with the assault rifle rapidly firing uncontrolled rounds as she was thrown backward from the recoil. The guard turned his gun on Margo. The uncontrolled rounds struck the guard as his body jolted and jerked. Jackson gasped and shielded himself from the uncontrolled burst of gunfire. Margo was thrown to the ground as the guard fell dead. Jackson patted his body for bullet holes, appeared relieved, and then hurried to Margo's fallen side. He took the rifle from her hand and pulled her into a sitting position. The ropes that once bound her wrists hung from her left wrist, bloodied from the knife she'd pulled from the dead man's neck to cut her bindings.

"You're insane!"

Margo threw her arms around his neck and clung to him while trembling from her ordeal and possibly to the life she'd claimed. Jackson held her against him and attempted to comfort her. He reluctantly pulled back and took a second to assess her for any injuries. He appeared relieved that she hadn't been hurt, despite her traumatized nerves. Margo suddenly met his gaze with a look of horror.

"Indy!"

"It's okay," Jackson announced with a reassuring smile. "Harlan has her, and Flynn is getting Liz back."

Margo appeared relieved while clutching her head, allowing her body to sag. She then looked back into Jackson's eyes. Without warning, she kissed him passionately and aggressively. Jackson appeared surprised but immediately returned the kiss. Flynn's voice crackling in Jackson's ear interrupted their kiss. Jackson pulled away and touched his earpiece.

"Yeah, Flynn," Jackson announced without awaiting his question. "I have Margo. She's, uh, safe."

"The lounge is empty," came Flynn's voice through Jackson's earpiece. "Liz is gone. Meet me at the watchtower."

"Be there in three," Jackson announced then looked at Margo's concerned expression.

"Something happened," Margo gasped softly.

"Just a setback," Jackson replied then pulled her to her feet. "Improvising is the air we breathe."

Jackson hurried Margo along the wall toward the watchtower, keeping her low and out of sight.

Chapter Thirty-eight

The watchtower was highly visible with the tied, hooded man dangling from the upper window on the second story. Jackson and Margo hurried along the wall and stopped near the tower doorway while remaining mostly hidden. Flynn suddenly appeared alongside them, startling Margo. Jackson didn't even flinch at his commander's sudden and mysterious presence.

"We have to find Liz," Flynn announced firmly.

Margo suddenly stared past them and held back her startled gasp. "Found her," she whispered and gave a slight nod across the courtyard.

Both men followed her gaze across the courtyard. Hugo stood behind Liz, his arm securely around her neck and a gun aimed at her temple. Tears streaked her face when she saw Flynn. Jackson and Flynn both aimed their assault rifles at the man holding Flynn's girlfriend captive.

"Flynn," she cried out softly.

Hugo gave her arm a firm jolt and dug the barrel of the gun into her temple. Liz gasped with alarm and remained still against her captor.

"Disarm the bomb, or I'll kill this woman!" Hugo cried out with anger.

Flynn stared at Liz with a look of concern on his usually tough face. As his finger flexed on the rifle trigger, his hardened look returned on cue. Jackson backed Margo against the watchtower wall, keeping her securely behind him while keeping his assault rifle trained on Hugo.

"Harlan," Flynn called out to nowhere in particular. "Disarm the bomb!"

There was no response. Flynn kept his eyes locked on Hugo holding the woman with the tear streaked face. Jackson uncertainly looked around, seeming surprised that they hadn't heard a response from Harlan. Flynn remained tough, but he twitched from the silence as well. It was unusual for anyone from Flynn's team not to respond when called.

"Harlan!" Flynn bellowed out with anger, the stress clearly getting the better of him.

Hugo stared back at Flynn with an air of arrogance on his face. "Something wrong, Stryker? Lose a man?" He then tapped his ear earpiece with his left hand while keeping Liz secured with his elbow to her shoulder. "Miles, bring Flynn's little girl." He awaited a response, but none came at his command either. Hugo's arrogant look faded. "Miles?"

Flynn and Hugo both looked slightly foolish awaiting response from their mysteriously absent men.

"Do you mean this girl?" Harlan suddenly called out from nearby.

Harlan appeared from the watchtower with Indy behind him. Flynn cast a quick, sideways glance at his daughter, appeared relieved to see her, and attempted to hide his smile.

"Are you okay, honey?" Flynn asked her, again focusing his attention on Hugo holding Liz across the courtyard. He didn't dare take his eyes or rifle off the man holding his girlfriend.

"I'm well, thank you," Harlan replied while grinning.

Flynn glared at Harlan and smirked. "Stop the counter on the bomb."

Harlan casually pressed a button on the remote control in his hand. The glowing counter on the man's chest high above them shut off.

"Now--the remote, if you don't mind," Hugo announced as he pressed the barrel into Liz's temple in order to make her gasp for dramatic effect.

"Liz first," Flynn demanded.

Hugo stared past Flynn. His expression suddenly dropped. Flynn cast a glance alongside him to see Harlan casually twirling the remote control out of apparent boredom. All eyes were suddenly on Harlan. Margo let out a slight gasp at his carelessness with the remote device. Harlan looked at Flynn with question then eyed the detonation device he twirled in his hand. He held the remote still and grinned with embarrassment.

"Oh, yeah, right," Harlan announced and held back his soft chuckle. "Sorry. My mind was somewhere else."

Hugo forced Liz across the courtyard toward the watchtower and closer to them. He forced her to stop almost halfway to them, which placed her fifty feet away.

"The remote," Hugo again demanded.

Flynn glanced at Harlan and indicated the remote. Harlan casually handed it to him. Flynn approached Hugo and Liz with the remote control, paused several feet away, and placed the device on the ground.

"I get the girl, you get the remote," Flynn announced.

Hugo released Liz and gave her a slight shove toward Flynn to throw her off balance. She caught her balance and hurried to Flynn. He pulled her into his arms and hurried her back to the watchtower and safety. Hugo picked up the remote control and grinned his pleasure.

"Kill them all," Hugo called out as he hurried across the courtyard to safety.

Hugo's men were suddenly seen perched on the walls behind him and opened fire. Flynn, Liz, and Indy dove to one side of the watchtower doorway, while Jackson and Margo leaped to the other side for shelter from the flying gunfire. Flynn fired back at the guards then looked at Harlan, who remained casually standing outside the door, despite the barrage of bullets. He wore a strange, twisted grin on his face. Flynn saw the look on Harlan's face from only a few feet away and appeared alarmed.

"Ah, hell no!" Flynn cried out.

Harlan held back his chuckle while grinning slyly and produced a second remote control. "On my mark..." His finger was firm against the button.

Liz suddenly screamed and leaped past Flynn for Harlan and the detonation device he held. The enemy fire ceased as if on command to the running woman. A foot suddenly struck Liz in the face, nearly tossing her through the air before she roughly hit the ground. Indy recovered from her fast, hard kick, straightened, and looked at Harlan several feet from her.

"You're right," Indy announced while cleverly raising her brow. "The coyote is evil."

Hugo started screaming for his men to resume firing. The men perched on the walls again aimed their weapons. Harlan appeared pleased with himself.

"Mark," he announced and pressed the remote control button.

Liz screamed with horror and looked to the dangling man in the tower. The remaining compound exploded systematically on both sides, rocking the ground beneath their feet. Guards were violently projected from the structure from the force of the explosion as the wall disintegrated beneath them. Hugo attempted to run for safety, although it was suddenly unclear where he would find any. Jackson appeared from alongside the watchtower and fired his assault rifle at the fleeing man, discharging a single round. Hugo fell to the ground while clutching his bleeding leg. Harlan frowned his disapproval, looked back at Jackson, and shook his head.

"Your aim sucks."

Jackson lowered his assault rifle and sneered at Harlan. "Some of us believe in taking prisoners," he announced. "Just because you don't understand the concept--"

"I took a live prisoner once," Harlan casually remarked.

Jackson allowed the assault rifle to fall into the crook of his arm and glared demandingly. "Oh, really? Exactly when was that?" he questioned.

Harlan grinned and proudly pointed up to the bound and dangling hooded man. Jackson eyed the dangling man then glared at Harlan.

"Yeah, and you're lucky. Flynn would have killed you if you shot our VIP prisoner," Jackson remarked.

"He's hardly a VIP prisoner," Harlan replied as he removed his Bowie knife from his boot.

Harlan approached the rope tied to the side of the building, suspending the man, and sliced through it. The hooded prisoner fell several feet to the ground, landing roughly near them. Liz scrambled to her feet near Indy and ran to the fallen, groaning man. Liz removed the hood to reveal her brother, Kale, who had been bound and gagged. She stared at her brother with shock and dismay. Flynn and Jackson were stunned to see Kale rather than their prized prisoner, Santiago. Flynn glared his annoyance at the group of people surrounding him.

"Anyone want to tell me what's going on?" Flynn demanded with hostility.

"Harlan's crazy," Liz cried out while helping Kale into a sitting position. She pointed demandingly at Harlan. "He tried to kill me and my brother!"

Flynn casually folded his arms across his broad chest and looked around with little emotion. "Anyone *other* than Liz want to tell me what's going on?"

"Liz is the coyote, Dad," Indy informed him.

Flynn looked back at Indy while appearing bewildered and baffled by the comment. "The coyote? I thought that was just some delusion manifested from Harlan's head trauma."

"No," Indy replied and sighed softly. "It goes much deeper than that."

All eyes were now on Harlan.

"I remember everything that happened the night of the compound explosion," Harlan announced. "I ran back inside to manually detonate the bomb..."

Chapter Thirty-nine

Six weeks earlier, at the compound...Harlan continued up the stairs in more of a hurry now. As he reached the top of the stairs, more men were heard thumping along the hallway. Harlan appeared annoyed by the continual setback. He darted into a nearby bedroom. As three guards appeared, one paused by the partially open bedroom door now swaying slightly. The guard hesitated, raised his assault rifle, and pushed the door open. Harlan backed across the darkened bedroom and lowered himself alongside the bed. The bedroom door slowly opened. A guard looked around the dark room. Harlan remained still, silent, and practically invisible. The guard turned and left the room. Harlan slowly straightened and listened to the sound of running feet in the hallway, becoming faint the further they got down the hall. Harlan relaxed and was about to head for the door when he looked at the framed photo on the nightstand. He picked up the picture and stared at the photo of Liz with a look of surprise that quickly turned to horror.

"Liz?" he suddenly gasped. As he stared at the framed picture of Flynn's beloved girlfriend, Harlan's expression turned to anger. "Son-of-a-bitch! She set us up!"

†

All eyes were on Liz as she clung to her brother while glaring at Harlan with loathe. Flynn folded his arms across his chest and raised a threatening brow. His unpredictable look was enough to frighten her. There was no mercy and certainly no love in his cold, harsh eyes.

"Would you care to confess?" Flynn asked in an oddly calm manner, although his chilling tone was unsettling. "You wouldn't want me to ask twice, now would you?"

Liz looked at the demanding eyes staring at her from every corner. Harlan's twisted smirk was enough to make her squirm closer to her bound brother. She looked back at Flynn and shuttered slightly.

"Santiago sent me to seduce you," Liz reluctantly informed Flynn. "He wanted me to find out what you knew about his operations. When the mortician died, Santiago secured our cover as his family taking over the funeral home business to place us in your circle."

"Why do I get a funny feeling Mr. Masters didn't die of natural causes?" Jackson suddenly announced.

Liz didn't respond and appeared ready to halt her confession entirely. Harlan crouched before Liz and her brother, smiled almost sweetly, and then rapidly pressed several buttons on the bomb vest panel. The counter continued counting down from five minutes, where it had left off. Liz gasped with horror and looked into Harlan's eyes directly across from her. He maintained his sweet smile.

"This state-of-the-art, hand tailored, bad boy bomb vest is my own design," Harlan informed her with pleasure. "I call it 'the imploder'. It'll only take out things within a few feet surrounding it."

Harlan grabbed her wrist, startling her, and skillfully zip tied her hand to the vest. She gasped and pulled against the plastic tie tethering her to the vest bomb. Liz instinctively met Harlan's sly, almost mocking gaze.

"You'll want to spill your guts, before 'the imploder' does it for you," he announced then casually straightened.

Liz appeared terrified and immediately started sweating. Kale stared at the counter on his chest and muffled a panic-filled cry for mercy. She immediately looked at Jackson.

"Yes, Santiago had the mortician killed so we could move into the funeral home," she quickly announced. She then looked at Flynn and attempted to plead with her eyes. "I'll tell you whatever you want to know, just stop the counter."

Flynn made a face and shrugged without uncrossing his arms. He maintained his broad stance while staring down at her. "I don't know, I think this will speed up the interrogation process."

"You must have been disappointed to learn Flynn wasn't much of a pillow talker," Harlan remarked.

She glanced at Harlan and appeared unsettled by his gaze. Her eyes shifted between him and the bomb attached to her brother. "Yeah, I found that out the hard way," she replied then fidgeted. "I had to improvise. Getting him to move me into his house was the perfect solution."

"Bitch," Margo muttered.

Jackson gave Margo a slight nudge to silence her, not wanting to interrupt story hour with Liz.

"You're doing fine, Liz," Harlan hissed softly, his devious smirk sending fear through her. "Please, continue."

She tensed while staring at the bomb then looked at those surrounding her. "Flynn let his location slip during one of our calls. I knew where he was going, so I warned Santiago here at the compound," Liz announced then hesitated and stared at Harlan. "From what Flynn had told me about you, I knew where you'd plant the explosives and told Santiago. He knew how to block your remote control signal. His men were waiting for your unit to show up that night."

"And the nurse?" Harlan demanded.

Liz tensed and drew a deep, shaken breath. "She was hired to silence you before you remembered anything from that night," she informed him. "When Flynn said you'd spoken my name before slipping into the coma, I knew you saw something that would link me to the compound and Santiago."

"And those men last night?" Indy suddenly asked.

"A last attempt to get rid of Harlan," Liz replied and again looked at the counter on the bomb. It was at three minutes and rapidly counting down.

Indy felt something nagging at her. "*Did* you try to poison Harlan with the turkey potpie?"

There was an odd hesitation, although the countdown may have been the reason. "Yes," she replied then gave Harlan a puzzled look. "How did you know it was poisoned?"

"You don't live as long as I have doing what I do without knowing the faint smell of poisons," he replied. "I guess my defense mechanisms took over despite my condition."

Flynn inhaled deeply while staring at Liz and Kale. His hand tensed on the gun's grip, carefully hidden within his arms across his chest. There was a tense moment of complete silence and several glances were cast at the intimidating man. Indy wondered if her father intended to shoot Liz or just leave her with Kale to implode together. She considered how she'd feel about it if he allowed her to die. She wasn't sure she liked herself after she realized her answer. Flynn finally looked at Harlan.

"You've had your fun," Flynn announced and forced a deep sigh. "Stop the counter."

Harlan again crouched alongside Kale and pressed several numbers onto the pad. The counter rapidly counted down from two minutes.

"Uh, oh," Harlan gasped softly and quickly straightened.

All eyes were suddenly on him and then the numbers counting down.

"Everyone should probably take cover," Harlan announced and took a few steps away from the tied couple.

Everyone screamed, ran several feet from the bomb, and dove to the ground, taking cover. Flynn dove on top of Indy, while Jackson tackled Margo to the ground. Liz screamed while fighting and clawing at the zip tie joining her to the vest. The counter reached zero across the entire line. Liz screamed and shielded her face.

Harlan stood three feet away and grinned. "Meep meep."

Flynn rolled off Indy, who groaned in agony from the weight of her father shielding her with his massive body. She could barely turn over. Jackson was quick to jump off Margo, who seemed particularly dazed from her rough tackle. All four looked at the evil smirk on Harlan's face. Liz stared at him while gasping and clutching her chest. Kale looked as though he'd nearly passed out. As the others slowly moved to their feet, Harlan chuckled with humor.

"You're insane!" Liz screeched while bouncing on her backside in an unsuccessful attempt to jump to her feet.

Flynn and Jackson simultaneously rolled their eyes and shook their heads with disgust at their comrade. Margo held her trembling hand to her head and just stared at Harlan.

"I'm going to kill him," Margo muttered. Her expression hardened, and she suddenly lunged for Harlan. "You bastard!"

Jackson caught Margo around the waist and swiftly returned her to where she originally stood. Indy frowned and smacked Harlan on the arm. He was possibly the only one who thought that was funny. Harlan yelped with surprise, gingerly rubbed his arm, and eyed her with annoyance.

"No sense of humor."

A jeep was heard speeding across the courtyard toward them, leaving a trail of dust. As the jeep came to a screeching halt, Nate looked around at the destruction. He met Harlan's gaze and grinned his approval.

"I see someone's feeling much better," Nate teased then removed the bound, gagged, and nearly naked Santiago from the jeep.

As Jackson cut the zip tie binding Liz to Kale, Liz and Santiago silently exchanged shameful looks and frowned. Flynn again folded his arms across his chest and arrogantly cocked his head while glaring at Nate.

"A little late, aren't you?" Flynn demanded.

"What are you talking about?" Nate asked with surprise. "I've been here for over forty minutes. Harlan said I was supposed to wait down the road for his signal. I assumed blowing up the rest of the compound was his subtle signal."

Jackson zip tied Liz's wrists behind her back and allowed Nate to secure her in the jeep with Santiago. They then carelessly tossed Kale into the jeep with them. Indy clung to her father's arm with a sympathetic look.

"I'm sorry about Liz, Dad," she said softly.

She knew he had to be feeling bad about being used by the woman he thought loved him.

Flynn looked at Indy and affectionately patted her hand on his arm. "Ironically, I'm not."

Indy looked at her father's hand and saw his wedding ring proudly displayed on his ring finger. She smiled gently and ran her finger over the wedding band. They exchanged knowing smiles. No other words needed to be exchanged. It was understood.

Flynn released Indy then glanced at Harlan and grinned slyly. "So you remember everything?" he asked in a tone that conveyed a verbal lashing was about to ensue.

Harlan drew a deep breath and nodded with embarrassment. "Yes, but there are things I wish I didn't remember."

Indy avoided looking at Harlan. She knew they'd eventually need to discuss their exploits, but it had been a long day, and that would be something she'd want to discuss with him in private. It could wait. Flynn placed his arm firmly around Indy's shoulder and glared at Harlan.

"Yeah, remind me to punch you later," Flynn muttered while hiding his smirk.

Harlan appeared stunned and cast a quick look at Indy as his mouth fell open. "You told him we'd slept together?" he suddenly gasped.

Indy's expression dropped. She felt her heart stop and her entire body twitch as the words left his mouth. Jackson, Margo, and Nate simultaneously whirled around and looked from Harlan to Indy. Her father's look hardened while staring at his comrade and best friend. Flynn's teeth gritted as he gripped Indy's shoulder to the point of hurting her. She squirmed slightly under his grip.

"You *slept* with my daughter?"

Chapter Forty

It had taken all night and a better part of the following day to secure prisoners on highly classified ships and brief bigwigs of the events that eventually brought down the remaining compound. Harlan was sent on his own, special mission to return his 'borrowed' plane to a secured military base that Indy wasn't supposed to know about. Although someone else could have returned the plane, Flynn left it up to Harlan, leaving Indy secretly suspecting her father wanted to keep some distance between them. Indy and Margo managed to catch a few hours' sleep on the flight home, but it took nearly the entire day to get everything straightened out. Despite being exhausted from their long day, Indy and Margo stayed up while waiting for the men to return from yet another briefing. Her father fondly referred to a mandatory second briefing as an 'ass chewing from hell'.

Indy and Margo sat at the bar with Roman while huddled over their drinks and a nearly empty pitcher of Cosmopolitans. All three looked a little disheveled but retained some enthusiasm to share their survival tales. Most normal people would probably be traumatized, but Indy and her friends viewed it as a chance to swap war stories with the commander. After their ordeal, sleep was the last thing on any of their minds. Roman shifted uncomfortably and gingerly rubbed his injured shoulder. His harrowing tale of survival intrigued both women, and the story wasn't about to get old anytime soon. Indy studied her friend and relived the entire incident at the funeral home. She knew she'd nearly gotten him killed, although neither expected to be ambushed that night. Indy still felt at fault, since she talked him into going to the funeral home with her without calling Sheriff Lerner for backup.

"I can't believe you're not dead," Indy announced as she stared at her friend. "Not that I was seeing straight, but I thought for sure he shot you in the chest."

"Thankfully Kale was a lousy shot," Roman remarked. "In my condition, I knew your best chance for survival was if I played dead and called for help."

"We're grateful," Margo replied.

"About that other thing--?" Roman announced, studied Indy, and appeared tense.

"Don't worry," Indy replied with a knowing smile. "I explained everything to my father. The FBI is going to handle the murdered nurse case. You and Harlan are in the clear." She studied her friend and noted his relief. "Liz confessed that the nurse was on Santiago's payroll as well."

"I can't believe those two played all of us like that," Roman remarked. "I mean, we all fell for their act. I thought Kale was my friend." He groaned softly and shook his head. "Your poor father. I can't believe Liz used him like that."

"I don't know," Indy remarked knowingly. "He seems to be handling it rather well. Only time will tell, I suppose."

"I'm glad you're both home safely," Roman announced and straightened with added stiffness. "Tell your father I'll talk to him another time. I'm a little worn out. I didn't get any sleep last night worrying about the two of you. Now that I know you're safe, I'll probably sleep for a week."

Margo grinned slyly while mocking his soreness. "Your first time being shot," she announced a little too cheerfully. "Guess that makes you a big shot around here, huh? Congratulations."

Roman hid his grin. "It's probably best if you don't bring that up," he replied then appeared uncomfortable. "Sheriff Lerner tore me up one side and down the other for not calling him for backup at the funeral home."

"Just an overly protective father figure, huh?" Margo teased.

"Are you kidding?" Roman blurted out. "He's been itching to fire that new weapon of his, and I ruined his one real opportunity. He's not happy with me."

"Jealous is more like it," Indy muttered to Margo.

"Well, we'll just keep that between us for now," Roman replied and slowly stood. He was obviously hurting more than he led on. "We can talk more tomorrow at lunch."

Both nodded and watched Roman head through the kitchen and leave through the back door. There was an odd silence between the two women as they fidgeted with their drinks. Margo finally sighed and looked at Indy.

"So," Margo began as she leaned on the bar and raised her brows with added curiosity. "What did Harlan say about what happened between the two of you?"

"Nothing," Indy casually replied. "We haven't had time to talk. My father was on him since he accidentally let it slip, and then he sent him to return that plane. I think he's purposely keeping him away from me."

Indy shifted in her chair and reflected on her indiscretions with Harlan. She wondered what the conversation would be like once they finally did discuss it. Eventually, her father would have to allow them some time alone. She snapped out of her trance and stared back at her friend. Margo sat quietly watching her, as if attempting to read her mind.

"Did you want to wait up for guys?" Indy finally asked her friend.

Margo grinned and raised her brows. "Hell, yeah! Jackson and I have some unfinished business to discuss."

"Oh?" Indy asked with surprise then noted the lustful look in her friend's eyes. She attempted to hide her smile. "A little gratitude for saving your life?"

"Nah, we're even with that," Margo casually replied. "This is just straight up sex for the sake of sex."

Indy held back her laugh. She never thought she'd hear those words coming from Margo's mouth, but she admired her honesty. Indy was sure Jackson wouldn't complain either.

"Are you sure you're ready for that?" Indy inquired. "I mean, you've been happily celibate since I met you in college. That's quite the track record." She hesitated and offered a timid smile. "You know Jackson can be, well, a bit of a whore."

Margo leaned closer to Indy and stared into her eyes. "I have two words in response to that."

Indy studied her friend with great interest.

"Five years," Margo announced firmly.

Indy held back her laugh. The front door was heard opening followed by arguing male voices. Indy felt her heart skip a beat. She didn't want to confront either her father or Harlan about what happened, but she wasn't looking forward to anymore awkward moments between them either. She needed to talk to Harlan and get things out in the open before it drove her insane. Margo, on the other hand, was enthusiastic for her fun filled evening of uninhibited sex with her own member of Delta Force. Indy envied Margo. She wanted to repeat that night with Harlan again and again, but this time, without the guilt. Sadly, there could never be anything between them. It was a complex situation exacerbated by friendships, loyalty, and honor among teammates.

"I didn't say that," Flynn was heard saying gruffly from the foyer. "Don't any of you ever listen?"

"We listen," Jackson announced, "but all we hear is blah, blah, blah, blah."

"Really? I'm carrying you know."

Flynn, Jackson, and Nate entered the bar area, saw both women were still up, and appeared slightly surprised to see them. Jackson smiled when he saw Margo and the seductive way she stared at him. It was obvious there was something already set in motion between the two. Margo grinned and stood without hesitation. Jackson pushed past Flynn, nearly knocking him down to reach Margo. He pulled Margo into his arms and kissed her passionately. Flynn and Nate watched the exchange while frowning. It was quite possible they were jealous. Flynn tore his eyes away from the kissing couple and shook his head with disgust.

"I'm going to regret retiring early, I know it," he muttered under his breath.

Jackson broke off the kiss and smiled lustfully at Margo. "Did you want to have a drink--?"

Margo took Jackson's hand and pulled him through the kitchen and toward the backstairs. "Good night," she called back to the others.

Jackson grinned and eagerly ran up the backstairs with her. All four watched with added surprise.

"Unbelievable," Flynn muttered.

"No one's getting any sleep in this house tonight," Nate muttered then turned to leave. "I'll be in the study having some brandy and a cigar."

Nate headed back for the foyer, leaving Indy alone with her father. They actually hadn't been alone since before his world was rocked by news of her indiscretions with his best friend. Although she was disappointed Harlan hadn't returned with them, it was probably best if she straightened things out with her father first. She wasn't sure what he was going to say, and she wasn't sure she really wanted to know. The feeling between them was awkward. Flynn poured the colorful drink from the pitcher into a clean glass and took a sip. He immediately made a face.

"God, this is like drinking pure sugar," he nearly gasped then glanced at her with a strange look. "How did your mother drink this stuff?"

"I can pour you a glass of whiskey," Indy interjected, wanting to please her father to keep from having their awkward conversation, and made a motion to round the bar.

"No," he announced gently and took another sip of the drink, making the same face. "I want to drink this."

Flynn remained standing while casually leaning both elbows on the bar. He stared blankly at his reflection in the mirror behind the bar. Indy watched him in silent concern. She didn't like that he didn't bring up Harlan. She hoped he hadn't secretly done away with him. Indy immediately shamed herself for thinking such things. He took another sip of the colorful drink while remaining transfixed on his own reflection.

"Did I ever tell you Harlan's last words before he ran back into the compound?"

Indy studied her father's profile and appeared curious. She didn't know where this was going, but at least he spoke Harlan's name without gritting his teeth.

"No," Indy replied and leaned on the bar facing him. "I don't think you did."

"He said, 'tell my girl I love her'," Flynn announced in a firm but soft tone. He finally looked at her.

She stared at her father and the expression on his face. Her mind was reeling from the words. "He always said I was his girl," she announced, feeling a little baffled by what her father had just told her.

He nodded while raising knowing brows. "Yes, I know that," Flynn remarked. "I never realized the magnitude of those words until last night at the compound." He looked back at his reflection in the mirror and appeared lost in another world. "If it ever came down to you or him; you'd win every time, you know that." There was a strange pause. He again looked at her. His look was serious and commanding. "Please, darling, don't ever force me to make that decision."

Her father finished his drink, set down the glass, and headed across the kitchen. She watched him slowly take the backstairs as if the world was weighing him down. Indy looked at the drink on the bar before her then frowned and allowed her head to fall into her hands. She wanted to cry. Her world officially shattered. There could never be anything between her and Harlan. Everyone knew it, but her father was the only one willing to say it aloud.

Chapter Forty-one

Indy entered the kitchen from the backstairs. It was a little after two in the morning. She was exhausted, but she wasn't able to sleep. Thoughts of Harlan and her father's words continued to play on an endless loop through her mind. As she approached the refrigerator, she noticed a faint glow coming from down the hall beyond the family room. The light had to be coming from the guest bedroom. She knew Jackson had reclaimed his usual bedroom connected to hers through the shared bathroom. Unfortunately, she knew this because she could hear Margo and Jackson going at it all night. Both were apparently making up for lost time. Indy veered away from the refrigerator and headed through the archway of the family room and into the connecting hallway in the back. She could hear sounds from the television as she approached the guest bedroom. She hesitated a few feet from the partially open bedroom door and considered her next move. Did she really want to have this conversation with Harlan tonight? It seemed pointless, since there wouldn't be any winners.

Despite that she decided against a confrontation at such a late hour, Indy was drawn to the partially open door and the light seeping out from it. The sound of the familiar cartoons caught her attention and momentarily sent panic through her. She hoped Harlan hadn't had a relapse of some sort. He hadn't been officially seen by a doctor since his memory returned to him. Something could be wrong. She owed it to him to make sure he was all right. Indy knew that was a lie. She wanted to see him! She didn't want to have that awkward conversation about their behavior, but she didn't want him pushed out of her life either. He was always going to be important to her, and she would always love him. Nothing was going to change that, and she couldn't allow her fears of what might be said to keep her from being near him. Indy drew a deep breath while feeling her heart pounding with anxiety. She gently tapped on the door. When there wasn't a response, she realized he might have fallen asleep with the television on. If he was able to sleep, she certainly didn't want to wake him. She felt her heart sink then turned to walk away.

The bedroom door opened, spilling light from the television into the hallway. Indy turned and stared at Harlan in the bedroom doorway. He stared back, sharing almost the same look she wore. He was still dressed, although without his shoes, indicating he'd only recently returned.

"Trouble sleeping?" Harlan asked gently.

"My mind is cluttered," she replied. "A lot has happened over the last two days."

"Happens a lot with new guys seeing action for the first time," he replied. "The mistake is thinking alcohol will help. Usually just makes the situation worse."

Indy felt her body start to relax as a smile crept across her face. "So what's the secret?"

Harlan grinned and motioned her into the room. She reluctantly followed him. He stood inside the bedroom, grinned, and indicated the cartoons playing on the television. She glanced at him and held back her laugh.

"Cartoons? That's the secret?"

"Worked for me for the last seventeen years," he replied then smirked. "Trust me; I've seen plenty of action. I know what I'm talking about."

Harlan approached the bed and cast himself upon it, landing in a sitting position against a headboard filled with pillows. Indy watched him only a moment then gently shut the door. The clicking sound was enough to catch his attention. He looked at her and appeared curious.

"Are we having 'the talk'?"

"Don't you think we should get it out into the open, so we can return to some sense of normalcy?" she replied.

"I've never been a fan of normalcy."

Indy resisted the temptation to laugh at his comment. He was back to the man she knew and loved, but she didn't want him to get off topic. He was good at changing the subject if he was attempting to avoid it. Harlan considered her comment while watching her across the room where she leaned against the closed door.

"Must we have this conversation with you standing ready at the door?" he questioned and indicated her hand clutching the doorknob behind her. "I'm thinking you're a flight risk."

Harlan moved over on the bed and patted the empty spot alongside him. Indy was immediately reminded of Christmas Eve, when he patted the bed, and she joined him. It was an action that led to the biggest mistake of her life, yet one of her fondest memories. Harlan suddenly hesitated as if reading her mind and smiled meekly.

"Oh, that's right," he remarked softly. "We had a little problem the last time, didn't we?" Harlan groaned softly and allowed his head to fall against the headboard. "I really screwed things up, didn't I?"

Indy knew she couldn't let him think that. She uncertainly approached the bed and joined him, allowing some space between them even though she wanted to curl up in his arms. He stared at her despite that she kept her eyes on the television. She feared looking him in the eyes. Her emotions were all over the place, and she feared any little thing might send her into his arms. Their situation was already tense. She didn't need to add to it.

"What happened between us that night wasn't your fault. I take full responsibility," she announced firmly, despite not looking at him. "You weren't in your right mind. I was, and I should have been the one to stop it."

"I don't see it that way. I was aggressive and persistent." He hesitated, drew a deep, tense breath, and looked away. "Maureen told me she was filing for divorce six months ago. Our marriage ended shortly after it began, I was just unwilling to accept it." Harlan shifted on the bed while avoiding looking at her. "We hadn't shared a bed in over five years." His frown told the bigger story. "I'm fairly confident she's been seeing someone else."

Indy looked at his profile and stared at him with surprise. Just another reason for her to hate Maureen. Maureen had everything Indy had ever dreamed of having, yet she was willing to toss Harlan out with the trash.

"I'm sorry, Harlan," she whispered softly.

"I was too, for a while," he replied then looked at her and studied her expression. His look turned serious and an awkward silence followed. He inhaled deeply and finally spoke. "I realize I wasn't in my right mind when I came on to you, but I want you to know that those feelings were real. You've been a major part of my life as long as I can remember."

"Growing up with you in my life is what makes this so hard," Indy replied softly while fighting the urge to cry.

Harlan groaned softly and looked at the ceiling a moment, as if searching for some divine inspiration. He finally looked back at her and stared into her eyes.

"That's not what I meant." He hesitated then turned slightly on his hip to face her and took her hand in his. "I loved you like a daughter when you were a child, and I loved you like a sister when you were a teenager. Then, when I returned home from a five-month deployment, I saw you at your high school graduation, and all that changed. That little girl was gone. That's the day I fell in love with my commander's daughter."

Indy stared at Harlan, and for a moment, she was unable to speak or even think. She wanted to throw herself on him and do things she was ashamed even to admit. As her brain began functioning again, she realized his words weren't those from a romance novel. There could be no happy ending for them. He was loyal to her father, and he would never go against his wishes. If anything, Indy was apt to defy her father more than Harlan was, yet she doubted she could betray her father in that way either. Her heart ached as they continued to stare into each other's eyes.

"I've loved you as long as I can remember," Indy finally replied with sadness. "I can't simply forget what happened between us." She caressed his hand holding hers and looked down while fighting her tears. "I just don't know where we go from here."

She looked back up and met Harlan's gaze. He stared back with a moderately baffled look.

"If this is about me returning to active duty, that chapter in my life is over," Harlan informed her. "I'm damaged goods. I can't go back to that lifestyle."

Now it was Indy's turn to feel puzzled. It was almost as if they were talking about completely different subjects. She sometimes felt Harlan thought she was capable of reading his mind. No one could read Harlan's mind. It was physically impossible.

"I wasn't talking about you returning to active duty," she replied while trying to understand the entire conversation. "I meant *us*."

"I was talking about us too," Harlan replied. "It's a simple question, Indy. Either you want a relationship or you don't. I'd like to stay here with you and the commander, but not if it's going to make you uncomfortable."

Indy's mind was suddenly reeling at the words coming from his mouth. Had she understood what he was saying? Was he willing to defy her father and resume their relationship right under her father's nose? Her heart was pounding in response. If she defied her father, would he really hold it against her? Her mouth opened slightly as if to respond, but she was having a difficult time convincing herself to speak as she stared into Harlan's eyes.

"I didn't know a romantic relationship was an option," she finally blurted out with renewed enthusiasm.

Her heart continued to pound. She was actually willing to do it. She was willing to go against her father to have Harlan in her life! He stared at her and remained slightly puzzled.

"Of course it's an option," he boldly announced. "Why would you think it wasn't?" Harlan hesitated then appeared curious. "Because your father is my best friend, my former commanding officer, and the only man capable of making my death look like an accident?"

Indy stared at him and held her breath. "Yeah, something like that."

Harlan smiled warmly and affectionately kissed the back of her hand. The sensation sent shock waves through her body. She couldn't take her eyes off him.

"After a long talk," Harlan announced then muttered, "and a little hand-to-hand combat, we came to an arrangement. I don't break your heart, and he won't tear out mine. Other than that, he reluctantly approved of us."

Indy stared at him with surprise as her heart continued to pound. "But earlier he said--"

Indy considered her earlier conversation with her father. *"If it ever came down to you or him; you'd win every time, you know that. Please, darling, don't ever force me to make that decision."* Her father hadn't been threatening to cast Harlan out if they started seeing each other, he was just asking her to be certain Harlan was the one. He didn't want to lose his best friend if their relationship didn't work. Indy stared at Harlan and fought her tears. She moved closer to him on the bed and placed her hands to his face.

"I don't want to lose you again," she whispered nearly down to tears. "And I'm willing to risk my father's wrath if it means we can be together."

Harlan kissed her quickly but passionately on the lips then pulled away and met her gaze with a broad grin.

"And I'm willing to suffer having Flynn as my father-in-law just to be with you."

Indy threw her arms around Harlan's neck and clung to him, fighting her tears of joy. He held her in a tight embrace with the promise of never letting go. Harlan pulled back just far enough to seek her lips with his and kissed her warmly but passionately. Indy kissed him back with added aggression, barely able to contain her rising passion. Harlan returned the aggressive kiss and gently lowered her to the bed.

The End

Other books by Holly Copella!
Reviews left on Amazon are appreciated!

"The Battle for Andrea Maria"

A cruise ship attack turns six survivors into overnight celebrities after they take credit for the heroic act of a stowaway who died saving them.

The cruise is just what Jess needed--a bit of harmless fun far from her daily grind. But what begins as a relaxing vacation turns into a desperate fight for her life when terrorists take over the ship and start piling up bodies. Teaming up with a mysterious stowaway, Jess attempts to send out a distress call but knows they cannot wait for help to come. If she or the few remaining passengers have any hope for survival, Jess must act now. The papers dub it "The Battle for *Andrea Maria*," but to Jess it is the moment she fought side-by-side with her enigmatic Romeo, saving the ship--and losing him. She thinks the story ends there, but really, the nightmare is just beginning...

"Insanely Deadly"

When the dead return to life, it's up to an admiral's daughter and a mildly insane, former war hero to save their small town.

Jetta Cross, a Navy Admiral's daughter, is tasked with keeping her father's comrade, a former war hero turned town crazy, grounded in the real world. Capt. John Hunter is still fighting the war in his head, where imaginary dead people are part of his world. When a viral outbreak brings about a zombie uprising, Hunter is left to his own devices. He must resume his role as a one-man commando unit in order to destroy the ravenous undead. With Hunter still fighting his own inner demons as well as the undead, the townspeople fear their zombie neighbors may not be the only threat. Stranded at the island's luxurious resort with a handful of workers, Jetta is forced to live up to her father's reputation and take charge of the deteriorating situation at the hotel. She must wage her own war against the infected before the government declares her hometown a total loss.

"Deadly Institution"

A town recluse suspected of killing his wife teams up with a young woman in order to stop a killer.

After being accused of murdering his wife, Konrad Asher turns his back on the town that once adored him. Ten years later, he still holds his grudge and the title of the most feared man in town. With the reopening of the burned mental institution, where his wife had died, former employees are now murdered one-by-one, throwing suspicion back on Asher. A young local reporter, Jacey, is forced to reveal her long-time friendship with the infamous recluse in order to clear his name not only in the recent murders but to exonerate him in the death of his wife as well. Will Jacey's relationship with Asher invite the killer closer to her? Or is the killer already in her life?

"Screenplays: The Island Collection"
"Jungle Princess", "A.L.F. Resort", "Brighton Island"

Discover how romance and fun in the sun can be downright *chilling*!

"Jungle Princess" is a romantic/thriller that leaves a teenage girl stranded on an island with two male shipmates and a creature of "unknown" origin. She soon discovers the island is home to an abandoned prison with several prisoners roaming free. What really killed over one hundred prisoners? And is it still out there--?

"A.L.F. Resort" is a romantic/thriller set on an island resort with Artificial Life Forms as the main draw. At this resort, all your fantasies come true...until a malfunction removes safety inhibitors on the A.L.F.'s. Zombies, biker gangs, and mobsters run amuck, turning fantasies into nightmares. A young reporter gets more of a story than she anticipates, but will she survive long enough to write the story?

"Brighton Island" is a romantic/thriller set on a private island. When the owner's niece brings her psychic friend to the mansion, his presence awakens the spirits' tortured souls. As the psychic attempts to solve the old murders, the niece is confronted with the possibility that she's next to join the mansion ghosts. Stranded on the island with a crazed killer, her uncle wages his own war to save them. Will his "shock and awe" tactics actually save them or get them killed?

"Reaper of Souls" A fantasy short story

A young woman must outwit an evil sorcerer in order to save her brother or become one of his minions forever.

Unwilling to believe her brother is dead, Reggie discovers an underhanded deal made with Kahn, a less than ethical sorcerer, who collects humans to serve as slaves in his kingdom. In order to rescue her brother from his horrible fate, she must complete his failed task or be forced to serve Kahn forever. After being transported to his world, Reggie realizes that even if she beats Kahn at his own game, she's at his mercy for him to uphold his end of the deal. All seems lost until Kahn's discontented, self-serving brother, Helsing, arrives. Can Reggie convince Helsing to help her? And at what cost?

"Death Displacement"

A grief-stricken man travels back in time to seek revenge on the woman who murdered his girlfriend but inadvertently falls in love with her.

Kane is about to marry the woman he loves. His life is perfect. A few weeks before the wedding, a vindictive woman from his girlfriend's past mysteriously arrives and kills her. He learns of a traumatic accident that happened five years earlier, which triggers Riley's hatred for his girlfriend. Distraught over his girlfriend's death, Kane uses an antique time machine to travel into the past in order to find and destroy the woman responsible. When he runs into Riley's younger self, he realizes she's not the monster she later becomes, and he can't bring himself to destroy her. With a little help from his oddball friend from the past, they formulate a plan to prevent the accident that sends Riley down her destructive path. Kane's plan backfires when he falls for the younger Riley. His new tortured existence is further complicated when future Riley, his girlfriend's killer, shows up with her own devious agenda that doesn't include him. Will he be able to stop the time ripple, which ultimately ends with his girlfriend's death? Or will future Riley take him out of the timeline forever--

"Dead Village"

After strange happenings isolate a small resort town from the rest of the world, nearly one hundred residents seek refuge at the closed hotel. Only eight survive the night. And that's just the beginning...

One day after the entire population of Fox Ridge Village disappears, a car wreck forces several unsuspecting crash victims to seek help at the closed summer hotel. Within the hotel, they discover the grisly aftermath of a brutal slaughter. Crash victims Vander and Devon, a reluctant clairvoyant, team up to solve the riddle of the "haunted hotel" and the mass hysteria plaguing the remaining survivors. By the time they discover the hotel's secret, they're already drawn into the hysteria. As the body count continues to climb, it's a race to isolate the source and bring everyone back to reality before they kill one another. Will Devon be able to communicate with the traumatized spirits before their fate becomes her own?

"Basement Dwellers"

A viral outbreak at a hospital leaves a mortician, sheriff, and coroner fighting for their lives against a horde of undead and the CDC.

After a massive car wreck leaves several survivors in critical condition at the local hospital, a surgeon uses experimental drugs on his critical patients and accidentally causes a zombie outbreak. When local mortician, Lexx, receives an infected corpse as her client, she becomes stranded in the hospital basement during CDC quarantine along with the local sheriff and the coroner. The infamous surgeon struggles to find a cure for his infectious blunder by using the other survivors as test subjects. Meanwhile, Lexx and the sheriff attempt to locate his missing sister, who's stranded somewhere in the battle zone that once was the emergency room. It's a race against time and the ravenous undead. Can they survive the undead before CDC sanitizes the hospital of all infection?

"Town Darling"

After surviving a brutal attack that claims the lives of those she loves, a young woman seeks revenge on a corrupt town.

Going back home is never easy, but for Casey, it means returning to her corrupt hometown where she barely survived a brutal attack. Accompanied by two family friends, she seeks justice for the night that destroyed her life. Her physical scars are nothing compared to her emotional ones, forcing the local sheriff to believe that the town darling is back for revenge. As the conspiracy for her revenge appears to be leading up to the coveted town fair, the sheriff is determined to stop her from fulfilling her vengeful scheme...but guilt over his role on that fateful night continues to haunt him. Will his desperate need for Casey's forgiveness be his undoing? Or will Casey's desire for revenge destroy them both?

"Witness Protection"

After witnessing an execution, a resourceful young woman attempts to disappear while being pursued by a hitman and a handsome federal agent.

A helicopter pilot, Jackie Remus, reluctantly agrees to go on a date with one of her clients, but her date is unexpectedly cut short when she witnesses a man being murdered. After narrowly escaping with her life, she is placed into protective custody. When the safe house is breached, Jackie makes a daring escape from both the hired killers and the handsome FBI agent, who wants to return her to protective custody. With a little help from her sly and crafty friend, Monroe, Jackie is convinced she can disappear until the trial. While on her journey to meet with her friend, she solicits help from a few shady but lovable characters along the way. Although she manages to stay one-step ahead of the hired killers, the federal agent remains in hot pursuit. Will Jackie reach Monroe before she's captured by the FBI and returned to protective custody? Or will the hired killers silence her first?

"Misfits, Inc."

A seemingly ordinary, young woman meets four misfits who claim she has given them supernatural powers.

While on a business trip to a remote island paradise, a bored secretary, Hailey, has her world turned upside down when her path collides with a psychic freak, Skyler. He attempts to convince her that they had met in his dreams, and she had chosen him as one of her four mystic warriors. After Skyler foresees a woman's death, they discover an unidentified creature has killed one of the guests. They are joined by a lounge pianist and a rich playboy, who also claim they had met her in their dreams. If Skyler's prophecies are genuine, the evil entity controlling the ravenous creatures needs to destroy Hailey to ensure its survival. Reluctantly accepting her fate, Hailey has to locate the last and most powerful of her chosen warriors, The Guardian. Their fate is in doubt when The Guardian turns out to be a self-absorbed, former cat burglar with a bad attitude. Can Hailey turn her company of misfits into an elite team of mystic warriors? Or will The Guardian's secret agenda destroy them all?

Coming Spring 2016!
"Witness Protection 2"
"The Return of Whiskey Tango Foxtrot"

ABOUT THE AUTHOR

Holly Copella has been writing since the age of twelve when her frustration at a book's poor plot drove her to author her own story. Over the last decade, she's written a number of screenplays, some of which she's now adapting into novels. Her fascination with zombies and other darker material lends an edge to her writing, which tends to lean toward horror. As a fan of Agatha Christie, she appreciates the craft of a good plot and the importance of creating significant characters.

Hailing from Pennsylvania, Copella lives in the Endless Mountains on a farm with her rescue horses and other animals. In addition to writing and reading fiction, she enjoys riding horses and traveling to Las Vegas and Disney World.

www.ingramcontent.com/pod-product-compliance
Lightning Source LLC
Chambersburg PA
CBHW061152170626
46809CB00003B/1059

* 9 7 8 0 9 9 7 1 0 6 4 0 4 *